MW00912812

Macie's Guide

to the

Odd, Strange, Bizarre, Unique,

Unexplained and Twisted

Macie's Guide

to the

Odd, Strange, Bizarre, Unique, Unexplained and Twisted

The Power Awakened

Melissa Carey

authorHOUSE®

AuthorHouse™
1663 Liberty Drive
Bloomington, IN 47403
www.authorhouse.com
Phone: 1-800-839-8640

Published by AuthorHouse   03/13/2012

ISBN: 978-1-4685-4908-9 (sc)
ISBN: 978-1-4685-4907-2 (hc)
ISBN: 978-1-4685-4906-5 (e)

Library of Congress Control Number: 2012901840

Contents

For my dreamers—Katelynn, Alex, Brayden and Nicholas

$\mathcal{C}$hapter 1

The bold letter C glared at her from her paper. It mocked her as if to say, you're nothing special; just another an average kid. She was always so close to tears now anyway and this was about to put her into major crying mode. Macie's grades were always good, but the Language Arts grades were especially important to her. She had put so much time into this paper, all the while thinking how proud mom would be, but earned a note in Mrs. Rich's handwriting: *creative attempt at the assignment* penned next to her name. Under what would seem like a compliment was the big, red capital C.

Macie may have been sitting as still as a rock, but inside her mind, thoughts were running wild. With her lips pursed shut and the graded paper clenched mindlessly in her hand she thought to herself. *This is wonderful. Just wonderful.* Then, she tried to talk herself out of caring. It was a good thing Mrs. Rich didn't hear her as she quietly mouthed the word, "whatever." It was on Mrs. Rich's list of "Things Not To Say In My Class." Macie could picture her teacher winking the first two fingers on both hands making quotation marks in the air.

Except, it didn't really feel like a whatever moment to Macie.

In the back of her mind, she heard a voice telling her to pull herself together. Papers shuffled around her. She didn't notice them. Time seemed to slow for her, but not for anyone else in the room. She couldn't get her thoughts away from the belittling paper in her hand.

Really, now. Can it get any worse? As if I don't already have enough bad days, I'm going to melt down over a stupid grade?

Instead of pulling it together, her mind went straight to the negative side, while her fifth grade class moved on.

Oh, of all the stupid things to get upset over today, Macie thought. Her short, brown curls bounced as she shook her head from side to side, as if she could fling the words out of her head.

Her thoughts wandered even more. It really shouldn't surprise me. I know they think I'm weird. Six months here and still no one likes me. Why would I think Mrs. Rich would understand any better than the kids in my class have? Half the class probably wrote the assignment the night before it was due. They're happy with their B's and C's.

Macie looked at her classmates as Mrs. Rich handed out row three's papers one by one to the students. A flash of white caught her attention. Melanie Lewis actually held her paper so everyone could see her A+ grade. Macie thought angrily that Melanie was the example that being popular means you also get to be the teacher's pet.

Macie was still lost in thought when she finally heard Mrs. Rich calling her name. The girls behind her were giggling. Beside her, someone coughed into his hand. Macie was sure she heard him say the word, "loser." And then, there was Mrs. Rich standing in front of her—looking right at her, as if she expected her to say something. Macie was confused and could feel the heat rising through her body. She knew that by now her cheeks would be red. Of course, she had no idea what Mrs. Rich wanted.

"Miss Graye, I called your name three times," Mrs. Rich said briskly, but with a soft tone in her voice. "Please put your paper in your folder and pass your homework to Miss Carter. Class, eyes up front!" Macie's teacher turned and walked around her desk at the front of the room.

Macie realized Annie Carter was turned around in her seat, waiting for the homework page. She handed it to her. For a moment, she almost thought Annie smiled at her. Macie thought with a sigh, she probably thinks I am the world's biggest dork. She's not really smiling. She's laughing at me without sound.

"Open your math books to page one hundred and sixty-two. Today we will review for this week's test," Mrs. Rich said as she turned to the chalkboard behind the desk.

The morning lessons continued as usual. Macie lived through the math lesson without any embarrassing moments. She even managed to raise her hand to answer a few problems.

Maybe the rest of the day won't be so bad, she was thinking as the lunch bell rang.

"Miss Graye, will you please wait here for a minute before going to lunch?"

So much for that.

The class was "ooohing" at her. Macie could hear them behind her. She watched them line up and leave with the other fifth grade class as she went to Mrs. Rich's desk.

Mrs. Rich seemed like a nice enough teacher. She was tough about getting your homework done and she gave enough of it. She had what she described to everyone as (always said with those finger quotes flicking in the air) "high expectations" for the students in her class. But, she was never really mean and always said something nice or encouraging to her students throughout the day. She gave praise for a good test, work page, or behaving in class. Still, Macie knew most kids did not want to be singled out by her. She felt like she had swallowed a hamburger whole, without chewing.

If Macie had known that Mrs. Rich worried about her every day, her throat might not have felt like it swelled shut. The teacher had known why Macie changed schools. She felt terrible about asking her to stand and introduce herself on the first day of class. She thought she should have known better how to handle Macie's situation. Macie had acted as if she had been asked to recite the Declaration of Independence and blindly looked about the room, stammering just to get her name out. When Mrs. Rich had tried to help her by asking how she liked living in the area, Macie had burst into tears. After that, she had stayed so quiet that the kids just left her alone. She noticed that Macie walked around shrouded in a haze most days. With just a little hesitation, Mrs. Rich spoke to Macie.

"Macie, I noticed you were very upset when you got your paper. Would you like to talk?"

Uh-oh. Oh, no. Even worse than being made fun of by your class, was being put on the spot by your teacher. Macie stood, for what felt like a whole minute, without being able to open her mouth. Then she heard herself speak without knowing what she was going to say.

"I just wondered why I got a C. I worked on it for the whole week before it was due. My dad even said it was the best story he'd seen me write in a long time." Macie caught her breath. She was amazed that she was able to say any of that.

Don't cry. Don't cry. Don't. Cry. She lowered her eyes and stared at the corner of Mrs. Rich's desk.

Mrs. Rich smiled brightly. "You're a really good writer, Macie. Your story was very creative and very well done." She emphasized the word story as she spoke.

Macie looked up at Mrs. Rich, feeling little bubbles of joy popping in her chest. It was nice to hear words of praise when she thought she was going to be in trouble. The bubbles popped quickly as Mrs. Rich continued.

"The only problem I had with your work was that it didn't follow the assignment. I asked for an essay on your personal career choice, not a story. You tried to do the checklist and include the how, why and where questions and what you hoped to accomplish. It was your career choice that made the paper too much fantasy and not enough fact."

Macie looked down at her feet. She knew she had stretched reality, but writing about becoming an author was too scary. No one, other than people in her family, knew that she wanted to become a famous writer. She wasn't ready for someone to reject her dream. In a way, Mrs. Rich had ended up doing just that without even knowing it.

"I did answer the assignment. I told you how I would become a mermaid and why I wanted to be one. I listed several things I hoped to accomplish and, and . . . well, my mom always inspired me to do neat stuff," she finished lamely. Macie felt a twinge of regret for not listening to that little voice that had tried to warn her not to write the assignment the way she did.

"And that's why I gave you a C instead of failing you for the assignment. You answered all of the questions, rather creatively I might add. But, the point of the assignment was to choose a real profession, not a made-up one. There's no such thing as gillyweed and you can't magically transform into a mermaid. Macie, sometimes you have to follow directions. It's part of learning." She paused, looking at Macie's trembling lip. "So, from now on for school assignments try to keep that in mind." She waited a few seconds before she suggested, "At home though, keep writing any ideas that come to you. Now, off to lunch with you," Mrs. Rich said as she smiled and handed Macie a late pass.

Macie wasn't sure how to feel so she agreed with herself not to think about it. If she had to admit it to herself, it wasn't really the grade that had upset her so much. It was just easier to believe that instead of letting herself think about what really made her so sad these days.

Of course, now she would have to walk into the lunch room late. That thought made her wish she had packed today. "Then I could just eat in a closet or the bathroom. Anywhere else but here," Macie mumbled to herself.

Instead, she walked in just as the last few people were getting their trays. It must have only felt like Mrs. Rich had talked for a long time.

I still have to find a seat, she thought with just a little bit of panic.

There was a spot next to Annie, who had already finished as much as she was going to eat. Macie had noticed that about her during other lunch times. Annie always finished eating before most of the other kids. Today, Annie was turned away talking to Robbie Primrose. Macie sat down next to her.

When Annie turned her head to look at who was next to her, Macie asked, "Is it okay if I sit here?"

"Yeah, sure," Annie said and then smiled before she turned and laughed when Robbie called for her to look at his best impression of a monkey.

Macie looked sideways at them, thinking that Robbie really did look like a monkey and that Annie was lucky to always have a place with friends at the table. She couldn't help feeling that it would be nice to be like them.

She hadn't felt this way last year at her old school. Macie had friends in school and never really thought about the kids who weren't part of her group. Everyone she knew, she had been friends with since kindergarten. They all seemed to wear clothes just like hers at her old school. Her friends there always liked the same music and went to the same places. They talked about the same things. It had never occurred to her that any of that could ever change.

Being alone really stinks, she thought miserably as she took a bite from her taco.

She finished her lunch quietly without noticing anyone else. No one noticed her, either. She thought about her old friends and her old school. Her old life. Life BMD—Before Mom Died.

Chapter 2

Macie could not remember a day where she was so relieved to get out of school. She packed her things quickly into her backpack. Waiting for Mrs. Rich to dismiss her and the few other students who went to the kindergarten classrooms to collect their younger siblings, she put on her purple jacket. Her little brother, James, was waving to her with one hand. He had a big smile on his face and a very large, painted flower in his other hand.

"Macie, Macie! Look what I made! Isn't it huge?"

"It's gi-normous, James." James mouth turned into a big, shining grin at her reaction. She took the picture as James reached his hand out toward hers. She looked over his art project while they walked to their bus.

"Wow, James! These are really great colors. I like how you put the darker ones in the middle and the lighter ones on the outside." Macie sounded just like her mom when her mother had complimented their arts and crafts.

"I know," was all James said.

Macie could see that James had inherited their mother's artistic ability. As young as he was, he could draw, paint and create faster and better than Macie. That was great for him, but she was more than a little jealous of his talent.

As they walked hand-in-hand with Macie carrying his flower, she felt that familiar surge of anger. It happened every time she thought about the things that she wouldn't get to share with her mother. The anger always returned like an ugly beast and made Macie uncomfortable.

It's probably because I had such a bad day, Macie told herself.

Macie sat on the bus only half-listening to her little brother prattle on about his day. Somewhere between his stories of Eloise getting caught picking her nose, "her finger was way up in there!" and how he singlehandedly won the ballgame after lunch, Macie replayed the last time she and her mother ever spoke face to face.

Macie sat on the bed, her fingers rubbing the old quilt over and over again. She wanted to be there, to stay forever. She also wanted to run from the room and hide.

"It isn't fair mom; this just isn't fair." Tears choked her throat and in a small whisper Macie said, "I don't want you to leave me, Mom."

Macie's mother motioned for her to lie down next to her. She didn't always have enough energy to speak now. Very slowly and very carefully, Macie cuddled in under the quilt and nestled herself on the pillow next to her mother.

"I know, baby. I know," her mother said softly as she stroked the side of Macie's cheek. "I tried, honey. I really did. I tried so hard for you and James and Daddy. I would do anything in the world to stay here with all of you, but it's my time to go."

They were both quiet for a while, comfortable with the silence. Being near each other would have to be enough. It always had been. Macie and her mother had always been able to feel each other's words and sense one another's feelings. They rarely noticed how much they didn't have to say to understand each other, but everyone around them took note at the bond they had with one another.

The silence eventually gave way to thought and tears took over for Macie as she thought of losing her mom and not being able to be near her like this anymore.

As if her mother was reading her mind she said, "Macie, honey, I will never be completely gone. Every time you think of me, I will be with you, somehow. You have to trust that I will always be near when you need me."

Macie couldn't respond. She listened to her mother's and her own breathing and laid her head on her mother's shoulder.

Macie's mother rested for a while. She allowed herself to breathe in her mom's flowery scented perfume on the quilt, and to look into her face. She wanted to memorize everything about her. She hoped she would never forget how her mom looked, how her voice sounded, how the light had once reflected off the golden strands of her long, silky hair.

So many questions jumbled together in Macie's mind. Many of them her mother had already answered. Some were selfish, like who would draw for her books when she was a famous writer? Other questions were technical, especially in the beginning. What is cancer? Why do you get it? Can I catch it, too?

Macie's mother had even given her a journal to write about it. She said by keeping a separate journal Macie could tuck it away when she didn't want to think about cancer anymore. That way, maybe her nightly journal wouldn't always be filled with thoughts of disease and dying.

There was one question left that Macie had not asked. As her mother opened her beautiful, but tired, green eyes Macie asked in a tiny voice, "Are you scared, Mom?"

Macie's mom hugged her as hard as she was able. In her always honest fashion she answered, "Yes and no. Yes, I am scared of what I leave behind. I'm afraid of missing out on your life and Dad's and James'. I'm worried how this happening when you are so young will affect the choices you make as you grow older."

She looked at Macie, waiting to see if she understood. She reached up slowly, and a bit shaky to wipe a tear from Macie's cheek. She took a breath and continued.

"Macie, I want you to know that I am not afraid of dying. I am at peace with the person I am and the way I lived my life. I know I have been blessed with two wonderful children whom I adore. I love your father so much more than I ever knew love could be."

She paused for a moment and closed her eyes, then said, "I have done exactly the things I wanted in life, although maybe not always in the order I expected them to happen. My paintings and the sculptures I create make people feel good. That has always made me happy."

Opening her eyes to look into Macie's big brown ones she gave her answer, "So, no Macie, I am not scared of what will happen now. If you are scared Mary Grace, my sweet little Macie, that's ok. Don't be afraid for me, though. Mommy will still know who you are, even from Heaven and I will wait there for all of you. No matter how long it takes."

Macie felt the weight of her pain and sorrow smash over her like ocean waves beating against the shore. Then it began to ebb away as she thought about her mother's words. She tilted her head up and kissed her mother's cheek.

"Mommy, when I grow up, if I have a little girl, can I name her after you?"

Macie felt her mother try to squeeze her. She didn't see the tear in her mother's eye, but felt it as it landed on her own cheek.

"Oh, Macie. My sweet, sweet Macie," she said softly. "If you grow up and still want that, it would make me the most proud and happy grandmother ever."

"MACIEeeeeee. C'mon Macie." James was shaking her by the arm. "Our stop's next." He pulled a disoriented Macie out of the seat as the bus doors opened for them to get off. "I said Caleb kept the frog in his book bag all day! Weren't you listening to me?"

"Oh, no! The whole day?" Macie asked. She was catching on to the story as her memory evaporated under his demands. She fixed her bag and tucked James' flower under her arm as she asked, "Then what happened?" She made great gagging noises for James' benefit the entire walk up the driveway when he told her how the frog got squished under Caleb's lunchbox. James giggled and told Macie that Miss Crenshaw had really gagged when she saw the frog guts all over Caleb's folder.

Chapter 3

"Gran, we're home," Macie announced to her grandmother while she dropped her book bag on the floor by the kitchen table. She began pulling glasses from the cupboards. As she poured iced tea for herself and James, Gran called out to them from upstairs.

"Your dad will be late again. There's soup cooking on the stove. Grab a snack."

Macie rooted through the fridge, grabbed some string cheese and two apples. She placed them on the table as she and James sat down to eat.

"I'm always so hungry when we get home," James spewed bits of apple across the table as he spoke.

"You're gross," Macie said. Then she agreed, "I'm always hungry, too.

It still felt weird calling this her home. Sometimes her mouth tripped over the word when she said it. This used to be 'going to Gran's house'. Now, it was home. The house she lived in; the one she returned to everyday. The place she slept.

Many of their things had been moved to Gran's old farmhouse. Clothes and beds along with posters and toys had been packed up when Dad decided to bring them here. He had explained it all to Macie and then she had caused a huge fight over the move. It was another one of those things that just wasn't fair.

Macie had shouted, "I don't want to leave my friends and my school!" She'd wanted to scream that she didn't want to leave mom's stuff either, but she wouldn't. She knew that it would just make them both feel bad.

In the end, Dad had won—partly because he was the dad and partly because his argument was better. He left for work before the bus came. Macie had tried to convince him that she could get herself and James ready. He said they were too young. He would also get home later than they would. Sometimes he would have to put in long hours getting ready for court. Then, he added in the fact that it wouldn't be fair to ask Gran to run back and forth to help him when he got called out at odd hours for work. In the end, they packed up a small box truck and moved an hour away from everything that held any tangible connection to her mother.

It wasn't like it was terrible at Gran's. Macie had always loved coming here to visit her farm. There were three horses named Charlie, Vanity, and Racer X. She loved the horses and while riding made her feel not exactly happy, it did seem peaceful at least. It was nice for Macie that Gran let her talk about her emotions in a way that her dad just couldn't. They played games together and shared stories with one another. Sometimes, Gran would get in a silly mood and turn on the radio or CD player so they could sing and dance around the living room. Occasionally Dad would join in, but not as often as he would have before Mom got sick. Mom could make Dad dance with just her laugh. Macie used to think of her dad as a big circus clown, always goofing around and making them giggle. For the longest time, she had pictured that being an attorney at the courthouse was like being a man in a striped costume with a big red nose, juggling balls in a circus tent. When she met some of her dad's lawyer friends, she'd thought how stuffy and formal they seemed. When she asked her mom about it she had answered that daddy was a "rare breed, indeed." Now he looked sad all the time. She could tell when he was faking happiness for hers and James' sake. Sometimes she felt like she lost both her parents the day mom died.

Macie couldn't say it was terrific here, either. Even though Gran tried to make them all feel at home, sometimes Macie still felt more like a guest than someone who actually lived here. It was different living here than just visiting had been. The rules had changed.

Gran had rules that they weren't used to and a routine that everyone had to strictly follow. Gran liked to know exactly what was going to happen and when, so she made sure everyone followed a schedule. Events that were not typical to the routine were written onto the dry-erase calendar that hung in the kitchen well in advance. Coming here before always meant lots of fun and playtime with Gran. Now there were more chores and work they needed to do to help her.

Macie finished her apple and threw away the core. She picked up the string cheese wrappers and deposited them in the trash. Eat only at the table and always remove your trail, Macie thought. While James headed off to find things to haul in his dump truck, Macie got out her homework folder. The 'C' paper rested in the keep-at-home pocket. She stuck her tongue out at it, took it out and turned it over. She ignored the paper and started her science worksheet.

Macie labeled the parts of the water cycle and started drawing the pictures that represented each phase. As she was drawing the next arrow, she heard the pitter-patter of Gran's bare feet on the stairs.

"Did you have a good day today, Macie?"

Macie shared a little of her day with Gran because it was expected of her. It was part of their routine. Macie barely remembered what her day was like once she got home, but had learned that Gran would not accept her saying nothing happened as an answer. They had settled into this system after school started. Macie did her homework at the kitchen table while Gran made or finished dinner. Then she found James' book bag, placing important papers on the counter for her dad to look over. Sometimes she helped Gran with dinner when she finished her homework in time. After that, they waited for dad to come home so everyone could eat together. If Dad was late, Macie helped James with whatever the K-kids were working on that particular week.

Macie retreated to her room before her dad got home. She did that a lot now. It had become part of her routine and the one thing that she hated most as part of "the changes." So often now, she was left with her own thoughts and not nearly as much time feeling like she was part of a family. She missed being with her mom. After-school time was always filled with laughter and silliness. Trips to the park or drives through the mountains, grocery shopping and errands, games of hide and seek and ones made up by her mother to keep them busy were all gone. The expectation that Macie could keep herself entertained and find things to do made Macie feel even more alone. Sometimes she only had herself to talk to and she wasn't very good company for anyone these days.

It was getting better. There were more days that were spent doing things together. What was also better was that her thoughts weren't always spent on sad and miserable feelings. While she was still known to tell herself how much it sucked (don't tell Dad about that word; he hated it, but honestly, what else could you say when your mom dies and goes away forever?), she was starting to remember things that she and mom did occasionally with a smile now instead of only tears.

It's a funny thing when you are left to yourself for long periods of time. Sometimes you can get so bored that time goes unbearable slow. Other times, you lose track of time so much that you get lost in thought and before you know it, hours have gone by. Macie read to fill her time and she was quite happy to be left alone to do that.

Sometimes, though, in the quiet of her room and in her mind, too many thoughts of mom rushed in and left Macie gasping for air. Once, not long after her mom had died, she had trashed her room. She'd thrown books from shelves, ripped clothes from the closet, tossed the blanket and pillow from her bed, and furiously flung toys across the room. That is, until she accidentally broke the glass in the frame that held the picture of Macie in her beautiful, white Communion dress standing next to her mother, healthy and smiling. They'd been positioned together to look at the colorful, stained-glass window with ribbons of sunlight streaming against the white of Macie's dress. The instant the glass cracked, the sound popped Macie out of her blind fury. She dropped to the floor, hugging the picture as tears cascaded down her cheeks. The bandage on her thumb from the glass that cut her was a sharp reminder for days that mom was never coming back. The leap between anger and sadness and back to anger was fast back then. In the months since then and with the move to Gran's, Macie had become numb to any emotions that caused any outward sign of her feelings. It was easier to go with Dad's answer that "some things just can't be explained and sometimes neither life nor death seem fair." It didn't really make her feel any better, but at least it was an answer of sorts in itself.

Today, though, in the solitude of her room she jotted her angst over the Language Arts grade in her diary. She felt a little better as she vented. She wrote until she could not think of one more thing to say. Her mind was clean and clear and utterly quiet for a moment. Then she felt the flash of words forming in her head and reached for her writer's journal. In it, she began writing the poem that flowed in her mind.

If one day you find a road that you've never seen before,
would you follow it along or ask for something more?
Would you try this new direction and just say 'come what may?'
Or would you stop yourself in fear and say, 'no I'd rather stay.'

While she was sure that Mrs. Rich would question her punctuation, she did not change it. She had a journal full of poems and stories. This one felt different. This one seemed to be telling her something. She read it over again. Her body tingled and gave a little shudder. The fact that it was on the last page of this journal made Macie feel that it had to mean something. That familiar tug inside her belly made her know it meant something.

Chapter 4

Dinner passed by uneventfully. Everyone settled into the living room after they finished kitchen duties. Dad was gearing up for a big trial on Monday, so he sat with a folder of notes on his clipboard and his iPad next to his leg. James was engrossed in an episode of one of those old shows on cable—the one with no mother and three fathers. Macie sat quietly on the couch next to him, barely watching while two of the characters, Stephanie and DJ, fought over DJ's diary as she drifted off into her own thoughts.

Macie jumped up a second before the phone rang saying, "I'll get it." As she walked toward the kitchen, the tone set for Aunt Julie started playing a Beethoven sonata.

"How'd she do that?" James asked. "I didn't even hear it ring." Gran shook her head, shrugged her shoulders, and frowned, but didn't answer him.

"Gran, it's for you," Macie called out. She met Macie in the hallway and went upstairs to take the phone call.

James attention went back to his favorite show. The episode was just finishing when Gran came downstairs and asked, "James, do you want to stay over at Aunt Julie's house on Saturday with cousin Andy?"

The reply was a loud "Yes!" that was followed by the question, "What day is today?"

"Thursday," Gran, Macie, and Dad, who was still looking through his notes, said in unison.

Gran continued, "Tomorrow is Friday and then it will be Saturday. Now, it's time to get ready for bed. Off you go."

Gran looked at Macie. "Aunt Julie wants to know if you'll go to the mall with her on Sunday when she brings James home."

Macie's bright green eyes sparkled. "Absolutely!" Spending time with Aunt Julie was about as cool as it could get. *She gets me*, Macie thought.

Macie talked with her aunt for a minute. "What time do you think you'll be here?"

"Be ready by one o'clock. We'll hit a few stores and see what new styles are out. Maybe we can find you a few new outfits."

"I can't wait! I miss you, Aunt Julie."

"I miss you too, dear. How's school going?"

Macie could have told her the truth, but instead replied, "It's good. I'll make sure I have my homework done before we go."

"I know you will. You always do. I have to put Andy to sleep soon, so let me talk to your grandmother again. I'll see you this weekend."

Macie told her aunt goodbye and then went to help James get ready for bed.

James wanted to read a story, so she picked one of his favorites about letters falling down all over themselves. James loved it when Macie paused and allowed him to say the letter's names and the words "boom boom" in his overly-loud voice every time they appeared in the story. He had the last page memorized and Macie waited while he finished the book. They were going over the back page with the alphabet as their dad walked in the room.

"Time for bed, champ," Dad said to James as Macie got up from the floor to get ready for bed. He gave her a kiss on the cheek as she walked toward the stairs.

Macie brushed her teeth and hair. The moon hung in the sky with an orange glow. She fell asleep thinking that it looked like a night-time sun.

When Macie woke the real sun was replacing the night sun. She'd had a dream that she would have to tell her dad about during breakfast. It had seemed funny to her and she thought he'd get a laugh from it, for sure. She wouldn't tell him that the dream came with a nudge. The only other time she'd used that word and tried to convince him that she dreamt something that happened that day, his face had turned the color of ash. He had walked away without a word.

This one was just plain weird though. She wanted to tell him about it and she didn't think that it would do anything other than give him a little laugh before work. She didn't think to question why she was in such a hurry to get to him before he left.

Macie went through her morning routine much faster than usual. Breakfast with her dad usually consisted of a ten minute window before he left for the office. Sometimes he was gone before Macie was out of bed.

Not this morning, though. There he sat in his suit and tie, his shoes always polished and so shiny you could almost see yourself in them. His hair sat evenly on his head. It was trimmed close enough to his head that when he combed his gel into it, it wasn't quite spiked and it wasn't combed flat. Mom had always teased him about being worse than a girl.

"I had a silly dream about you last night, Dad." Yep. Silly. That was a word no one could get upset about.

"Oh yeah, pumpkin-head? What about?"

"Well, it was so normal but, then it wasn't. It was like it could really happen." Oops. *What happened to keeping it silly?*, she asked herself.

A look passed from Gran to Dad that Macie couldn't quite make out. It was gone so fast that Macie thought she might have imagined it. At least, she hoped she'd imagined it. She launched into her description.

"You are sitting in a room, waiting for a man to show up. He seems to be important because you said something about a key. I guess he had a key or he needed one. You stand up and start walking around, kind of like pacing. Then you realize you have no shoes on. You look down and see you have on one blue sock and one black sock. When you notice that, you say, 'no wonder I've been feeling unbalanced all day.' Then you look at the door."

Macie stopped for a minute. Then, with a chuckle, her dad asked, "Well, did the man ever show?"

Macie grinned and then looked into the air, picturing the dream. "No, he never did. In the next part of the dream a lady comes in and says he can't make it because he has to pee on the side of the building."

James burst out laughing and Macie giggled, too. Dad chuckled again and then looked thoughtful. His shoulders relaxed.

"That is a silly dream. Although, I am meeting with someone today for next week's case. I'll have to make sure he knows where the bathrooms are," Dad said as he winked. James erupted into a fit of laughter again and then realized he had to use the bathroom, too. He ran down the hallway.

Dad got up and grabbed his overcoat. "Guess I better make sure both socks are black," he teased.

He bent over and grabbed his pants at the knees. When he pulled both pant legs up over his shoes he and Gran inhaled, while Macie exhaled so fast she almost whistled, all of them at the same time. One sock was black, but the other was blue.

It took a beat before he said anything. "Well, what do you know?" he mused as he went upstairs to find new socks.

Gran looked annoyed, glared at Dad's empty seat, and then abruptly got up to busy herself with the breakfast dishes. It didn't take much to realize Gran was upset with her for seeing the socks in her dream. She didn't look at Macie or say another word.

Macie picked up both book bags and met James on his way back to the kitchen. "Hurry up or we'll be late for the bus," she said, even though they had at least ten minutes before it was due at their stop. It would be worth listening to him whine about standing there so long just to get away from the house and Gran's sudden irritation.

"We're leaving for school now," she called out as she herded James to the end of the drive

How weird that going to school will be better than being here today, she thought. Then she smiled as she remembered exactly how much better school was going to be.

Chapter 5

Friday's were Macie's favorite day. Music day, pizza day, and the last day of the school week all rolled into one. Today was an even better Friday than usual because there was a special assembly. One of Macie's favorite authors, Ella Creed, was coming to the school. Holy wow, Macie thought again, she's going to be in my school! She giggled with excitement. She had that sensation that made her whole body vibrate as she thought about how lucky she was to be at this school at the right time. Macie and James had all of her books. James loved to look at the pictures. Hers was the first book Macie had read when she started reading chapter books.

Every time she pictured the assembly, she felt a rush of energy like bees buzzing all around her. Macie was so excited to learn everything Ms. Creed did to become a success. Macie had told herself so many times that she wanted to be just like her. A thought floated in her mind. Maybe I'll be able to find new ideas to write about today.

She tried to pay attention to Mrs. Rich and her lessons. Luckily the few times her mind wandered, Mrs. Rich did not call on her for an answer. Unfortunately, she did not hear her ask the class to line up for music. Everyone had noisily shoved their chairs back before Macie realized what was happening. Her head jerked up suddenly. A few of the girls behind her snickered at her while she walked to the back of the line.

Macie managed to make it through music class without an embarrassing moment. Mr. Meloni was a great teacher, although she thought he sometimes was obsessive about his subject. Today he said something about a Dorian mode. At first she thought he'd said DeLorean, like the car in those old *Back To The Future* movies that she and James watched sometimes with their Dad. Mr. Meloni seemed to think it was neat, but Macie thought it was . . . she giggled to herself . . . Bore-ian.

Their class went straight from music to lunch. It was in the lunchroom that things went strangely bad for Macie. On her way out of the lunch line doors, Macie felt the hair on the back of her neck rise. The skin there felt as if it were being pricked by a hundred needles at once.

Later she would write in her diary that what happened flashed before her eyes a second before it really occurred. She took two steps toward the fifth grade lunch table and slid on someone's spilt chocolate milk. One minute she was standing and the next she was on the floor with her pizza upside down on her shirt. The silverware from her tray slid across the floor and her salad had taken flight on the downward crash. Now a piece of lettuce stuck to her hair, as well as Penny Oliver's. Penny had the misfortune of being in front of Macie as they walked out of the lunch line.

For a moment that seemed more like an eternity, the entire cafeteria was silent. Within an instant the crowd of fourth, fifth, and sixth graders broke into a simultaneous, elongated, and predictable "ooohhhhh" that was followed by deafening laughter and some random clapping.

Mr. Dunn, the gym teacher, who was on cafeteria duty, came to help Macie. Most of the lunchroom went back to their lunch and conversations, although Macie could feel a few people still staring at her.

She wanted to burst into tears, but that would surely draw more attention to her. Mr. Dunn made sure she wasn't hurt and then he told her to ask the lunch ladies for another tray.

Macie did and this time walked carefully while searching for a seat with her class. She did not look at anyone. Instead she focused on the stain on her shirt. As she was staring at the saucy imprint, Macie overheard Penny talking to Maya and Kaylie.

"She tripped because of her big, ugly shoes," Penny sneered, making Kaylie and Maya laugh.

"Yeah," Kaylie joined in. She narrowed her eyes as her top lip curled up. Her nose wrinkled as if she smelled dog poop as she said, "She's such a disaster. And now you have salad dressing on your shirt. She's got some nerve."

Maya was a little on the shy side. She looked nervous as she said, "You really can't see the spot now." With a slight pause, she continued, "I feel bad for her. Every time someone falls or drops a tray, everyone laughs. I would hate that."

"Well, I don't care. Not one bit," Penny ranted. "She thinks she's so much better than us. I'll bet she doesn't think she is so great now with her pizza shirt. What a freak!"

"Come on, Penny. Forget her. It's almost time to line up," Kaylie said. Kaylie always made sure that Penny knew what was happening next. Penny liked to be first for everything. Her friends realized she was a lot nicer when she got her way and spent a lot of time making sure she did.

Macie wasn't hungry anymore, but she pretended to eat by sliding her food around and cutting up her pizza. She kept her eyes on her tray as if she was focused on a difficult task. She hid her face so that no one could see her tears. She waited until the last moment possible to dump her tray contents in the oversized garbage cans lining the front of the cafeteria. She carefully avoided looking at anyone as she settled back into her seat at the end of the table. Luckily, the bell rang to dismiss her from her misery.

Being seated on the end, Macie had to be the first in line. She led her class from the lunchroom. "Great," she muttered softly, "Now if I fall again, they can all just walk right over me."

Mrs. Rich was standing in the hall, waiting for her class. When she saw Macie she gave a look of surprise, followed by one of concern.

Quietly, she asked, "Miss Graye, what happened to you?"

"I slipped on the way to the table and my tray just . . ." All of the sudden, Macie was glad she was in the front of everyone as fresh tears glistened in her eyes.

"Why don't you go to the nurse's office and use Mrs. Murphy's bathroom to clean up. Ask Mrs. Matthews in the office if they have an extra shirt from lost and found. Take your time. We're only going to play a game of Sparkle while we wait for the assembly to begin."

Macie put her head down hoping that if she didn't look at anyone no one would notice her stained shirt. It helped her avoid any glares that Penny might be throwing her way. I have got to stay away from her, Macie thought as she wondered what it could be that had Penny acting like Macie was her mortal enemy since the day she got here. Shaking her head as if to loosen some memory of what she could have done to Penny, she came up empty. She barely talked to anyone and she didn't talk about anyone, either. She'd headed off to the nurse's office and gave up trying to figure it out once she walked through the door, where she found Mrs. Murphy finishing a phone call. A small child was lying on the cot. He looked white and pasty. She headed past the cot toward Mrs. Murphy.

"May I use your restroom, please?"

Mrs. Murphy, taking one look at Macie's clothes, simply nodded while attending to the now-moaning child.

"We may need to get in there, so be listening for us at the door," Mrs. Murphy warned as she crooked her head in the direction of the boy on the cot.

Macie closed the heavy door as gently as she could and then started washing her hands and face. Her hair had some dressing streaked through it. She ran a paper towel under the water and tried to rub it out. Her right leg had a little sauce on it and her skirt had a grease spot.

"This was supposed to be a great day?" she said in the most sarcastic tone to the girl in the mirror. To make it worse, she looked at the reflection of her shirt and realized that she'd forgotten to ask for another one.

Chapter 6

Macie went through Mrs. Murphy's door and walked into the office. A woman with beautiful, long, dark hair was talking to Mrs. Matthews. She stopped talking when Mrs. Matthews looked up at Macie.

"Can I help you, Macie?" She smiled her famous smile. Everyone in school made comments on how Mrs. Matthews is always happy.

Macie told the lunchroom story, feeling a little better now that she'd had time to get away from her class and everyone who had seen her very ungraceful fall. Everyone who had made her feel stupid and ashamed. It was nice to be clean again, too. She looked at her shirt. Well, almost clean.

"Mrs. Rich sent me here to see if you have a shirt I could borrow from lost and found," Macie completed her request by telling her slip and fall story, giving Mrs. Matthews the reason for her visit to the office.

The pretty lady with the long hair turned to Macie and said, "Oh! I remember that happening to me in school. Only it was chicken and gravy for lunch and the mashed potatoes were stuck in my hair all day!" She laughed a pleasant, happy laugh and then said, "I'm Ella Creed. It's very nice to meet you. Macie, is it?"

Macie could have dropped to the floor from her nervous excitement. Had she not been standing next to the office counter, she just might have. She leaned her elbow on it for support and realized her mouth was hanging open in a complete 'O' shape.

The first thing she said when she was able to think again was, "your hair is different than the picture on your book covers. It's longer." As soon as it was out of her mouth she wanted to bang her head on the counter in embarrassment.

Ms. Creed laughed, "Over the years I have changed my look a few times." She paused and then said, "I guess that means I have a fan then."

"Oh, yes! I love your books. My brother does, too. He's in kindergarten, so not the chapter books. I read them to him sometimes, though. He loves reading about the little dog in the big, big world."

"That's nice that you read to him. Did you bring one for me to sign?" Ms. Creed asked her

Macie's cheeks felt flushed with excitement, then frustration. "I did! It's in my classroom. I may not make it there before the assembly now."

"Don't worry. If your teacher allows you to bring it up here after the assembly, I'll wait to sign it."

Macie's face lit up with a huge smile. "Thank you, Ms. Creed! I will. I want to know everything about what you do. I want to be an author, too, when I grow up," she blurted out quickly, surprising herself.

"That's wonderful. I always love to meet an aspiring author. I have lots of ideas to share during the assembly. There should be time for questions at the end, if you have any," she told Macie, smiling again.

"Okay. I can't wait!" Macie's face was lit up with excitement.

Mrs. Matthews interrupted them, "Macie, here's a nice shirt that I found. It matches your skirt. Hurry up, though, because Mr. Sweeney's starting to call the K-kids to the assembly."

Just then, Macie heard the principal's voice coming from behind her and from over the loudspeaker in the hallway. She reached for the shirt and raced into the nurse's office in time to hear pasty kid vomiting in the bathroom. Macie stepped behind a privacy curtain and switched shirts. She looked at the stained shirt in her hand, thinking how lucky it was that she had gotten pizza all it. She now felt that falling in front of a roomful of students was the best thing that could have happened to her. It was made even more wonderful by the fact that she shared a similar story with her favorite author.

The assembly was the best thing Macie had been to in a long time. She couldn't remember ever feeling this excited about anything. Ms. Creed had always been a favorite author of Macie's because of the way she wrote her books. She now held a special place in Macie's heart for how she talked about writing her books. Macie couldn't believe that an author would be so willing to share her secrets and the "process" as Ms. Creed had described it. She had even called on Macie twice when she raised her hand with questions. When Ms. Creed said, "I hope to read one of your books, one day," Macie had beamed from ear to ear—before turning seven shades of red and trying to hide from the students and teachers who were now looking at her. She left the assembly floating on air and happier than she'd been in months.

Macie asked Mrs. Rich if she could take some paper out to the playground. The assembly was not only amazing, but informative, too and she wanted to make some notes. Macie's head was still floating in the clouds. She didn't notice the other students running around. She didn't hear their voices as they chased, ran, slid, swung, and tagged. The playground had become an oasis in her thirst to remember all that she had heard. She drank in the fresh air and drove her attention to digesting the wonderful talk she had heard. She looked at the scrolled and looped signature of Ms. Creed on the inside cover of her book and the special note she had written just for Macie.

Ms. Creed spoke about why she became a writer and how she decided what to write about. She also explained the process from putting your first thoughts on paper and all of the things that happened between that first moment and finally getting the book into the store. Macie didn't want to forget any of the important things. She sat cross-legged on the ground under the big oak tree writing snippets of information and quoting things that felt important to her. She was so inside of her own mind, she didn't notice that anyone had approached her.

Penny sneered at her and Macie looked up as if she had been smacked. "I hear that writers who can't get A's on their assignments only get jobs in garbage dumps. That way when they write, their stuff is already in the trash where it belongs."

Macie wanted to crawl into a hole when she heard Penny's mean comment. She was stunned and speechless. Finally her mind kicked in and she stood up. A few of the kids made sounds, wondering if there was going to be a fight.

Macie hadn't had any real knock-down, punch someone kind of fight feelings in her, and she had even less these days. What was the point? She didn't want to give Penny any more reasons to lash out at her. She tried to take what she felt her mom's advice would be and find a way to call a truce. At best, she might be able to get Penny to leave her alone. At worst?

Well, let's not think about that, she told herself right before she spoke.

"Listen, Penny. I'm really sorry about what happened in lunch today. I didn't mean to . . . it was an accident. I really did just slip. Of course, I would never have done that on purpose." She hoped that just addressing the issue would help Penny see that she was being extremely nasty over something that could have happened to anyone. It didn't occur to her that Penny could really hold a grudge.

"Don't! Don't even apologize to me, you snobby little brat. Don't bother." Penny turned and walked to the other side of the playground, her troop following her. Everyone else walked away when they saw that nothing big or exciting was going to happen.

Macie was left in complete shock with no answer to why Penny would treat her like this. It couldn't possibly be over an accidental splattering of food. She watched Penny march off with her little club wondering what she had ever done to be called a snob or a brat.

Resigned to being confused and refusing to let Penny ruin what was the first day she had ever been happy to be at Lakewood Elementary, Macie folded her papers and headed toward the school. Mrs. Rich called for her class in the middle of her fourth step. She was careful not to fall in line anywhere near Penny or her friends. It must be nice to have friends, she thought as she fell into line behind Annie Carter.

When they took their seats in the classroom, Mrs. Rich reminded them to pack up folders and books. Thankfully, it was time to go home. "Don't forget your writing assignment. Your typed copy is due on Monday. You'll be adding in the visual aids with Mrs. Harbaugh in computers on Tuesday."

A unison groan was the class answer.

Mrs. Rich chuckled, "Well, now. Computers aren't just for games, you know. Everyone presents the final version in class on Wednesday. Maybe you can all think of how to apply something you learned today at the assembly."

With that final thought, she dismissed them to their appropriate destinations. Students talked with each other, making plans to call and text each other during the weekend or get together for sleepovers if their parents allowed it. For yet another moment, Macie felt sad for herself and her lack of friends. Then she focused on her trip with Aunt Julie and how much fun it would be. She whispered to herself, "It would be much nicer to find a friend to shop with."

$\mathcal{C}$hapter 7

Happy to be home again, Macie flowed through her after-school routine. Friday meant a break from homework after school. She and James played a game of Go Fish before dinner. She was anxious to write more about the assembly before she forgot anything, but Gran seemed preoccupied and a little grumpy this afternoon.

Tonight they were eating without Dad. It wasn't unusual, right before a big trial, for Dad to stay late at the office. He often said being at the District Attorney's office made him "responsible for being responsible." Macie had heard this so many times when the family complained about missing him. There were times he was even called out by the police if a particularly bad or odd thing happened and they needed someone from his office at the scene of the crime. He took it in stride and when they complained about having to change their plans, he would just say, "It's how the system works."

Dinner was a family favorite tonight. Everyone took large helpings of meatloaf and mashed potatoes with green bean casserole. A fresh-baked cherry pie smell wafted through the air making them hungry for dessert.

Macie told everyone her pizza story during dinner. She had gotten over the embarrassment once she heard Ms. Creed's story. She was still puzzled and annoyed that Penny was being so awful to her. She asked Gran why she thought that Penny would be so nasty. James offered to beat up Penny for Macie. Gran thought that maybe Penny was embarrassed and it was easier to make fun of Macie.

"Maybe she needed to put the focus on you because she didn't want anyone to make fun of her," Gran said.

Macie disagreed, already knowing there was more to it than that. She realized this wasn't the first time she had felt Penny's anger at her. She could feel so much tension whenever Penny was anywhere near her. The more she thought about it, the more it seemed that Penny always had been stiff and sullen around her. The little nudge inside her stomach said she right. She didn't really want to talk about it with Gran anymore, so Macie nodded her head as if she agreed with her.

"What did you say Penny's last name was? I wonder if I know her parents," Gran mused.

"Oliver. Penny Oliver."

"Oliver? That name sounds familiar. Hmmm."

The phone rang, thankfully interrupting Gran's line of questioning and she talked to Aunt Julie while they all cleared the kitchen of its dinner aftermath. Macie and James placed their dishes in the sink. Macie could hear Gran talking.

"No. He had to stay late tonight. His key witness didn't show today or something like that. They were going to make him take a . . ." Gran started to say something else, but paused as she looked at Macie. She directed her attention to Macie who was still clearing the table.

"I've got this Macie. You and James can go find something to do."

Macie was happy to be free from kitchen duty for the night, even though it seemed odd that Gran would let them off the hook from chores.

James headed to the living room and flipped the channel to his favorite cartoon show. The sponge dude was about to send a rocket into space. James flopped on the couch and Macie headed upstairs.

"Time to write," she said to the air.

She shouldn't have been worried about remembering the talk Ms. Creed gave. The minute she opened her writing journal it was as if the assembly had just begun. The words flowed from her inner ear right to her fingers. As she wrote, she heard herself repeating as her fingers worked to catch her thoughts. Macie could clearly hear the sound of Ms. Creed's voice as if her mind had recorded the assembly and given her a rewind button. She continued right where she left off at the playground,

Macie underlined some and then highlighted others of the best parts of the assembly. She whispered Ms. Creed's words while she wrote them next to the number one on her paper, " . . . said she 'always starts a book with something she sees or knows.' Two," she said as she paused to collect her thoughts. She wrote next to the number two, take a real life experience and create something new from it.

She wrote the letter A under the number two, followed by 'Add to it'. Next to the letter B she placed underneath, she wrote, 'Define It'. She worked on her list a little longer—pausing while she wrote out her notes, rewinding her thoughts, highlighting and summarizing.

Even though she felt like she was giving herself homework from the assembly during a weekend and that made her slightly crazy, she didn't care. She finished her notes.

"I don't care. This is fun to me," she said to the air again as she looked over her notes and made changes to correct her five numbered points.

Macie was putting away her journal as James burst into her room.

"Wanna play monster trucks with me, Macie?" He held out a yellow truck with huge black wheels and a big green snake painted along the sides.

"Sure. I'll bet I win though," she teased.

She and James jumped monster trucks over a ramp he that had set up in his room. It was made from a few cars in various heights that were placed under some of his books. Each time they started a new round, James named the goal for the jump. The goals ranged from making the truck the fastest or highest to traveling the farthest and landing on its wheels.

They'd gotten smart after the first time they raced the trucks. Dad and Gran had not been amused by all the noise. Now they used blankets on the floor to absorb the crashing sounds.

This was where their dad found them. James and Macie were poised at the ramps, ready to make the next jump. James had lined up all of his metal cars side by side. The truck that jumped over the most cars was the winner of this match.

Dad cleared his throat and James nearly flew up from the floor to squeeze him around his waist. He tossed James up in the air and laughed.

"Hey, how's my buddy today?"

James buried his face in Dad's shoulder and said a muffled, "good."

"And how about you, Mace?" he asked as he ruffled her dark, brown hair. Gran said you had a rough day. Need to talk?"

"No, I'm okay. I guess." She paused for a second, before switching topics. "The assembly was awesome!" The word awesome came out with a sing-song voice. Macie knew she wasn't exactly okay with the Penny thing, but Dad wasn't the person she really wanted to talk to about it. He hadn't been great in the school-girl angst department before and now that mom was gone, he didn't help Macie talk much about anything.

"Well, maybe later then, kiddo. If you want to talk, I'll listen. I'm glad you enjoyed the assembly." Macie realized this was a big step for him. He hadn't offered to talk about much of anything since they moved here. Maybe. Maybe she could cut him a break and let him try again.

Something seemed different about the way he looked at her, but Macie couldn't quite figure out what it was. She didn't understand why he was looking at her that way at all. Her stomach lurched and she knew there was more information to be shared with her dad. She had a feeling she'd find out exactly about what soon enough.

Chapter 8

The evening passed quickly and quietly. They sat as a family and played seventeen rounds of I Spy because James kept picking his things right before he gave the answer, dragging out the game. Then they watched a funny movie together. Dad laughed with Macie and James. They cuddled together on the couch until James fell asleep in Dad's arms. While he carried James up to bed, Macie began her bedtime routine. She started in the bathroom and ended in her bedroom where she put on her pajamas and turned down her bed.

She heard her dad's footsteps coming up the hall. She looked up as he peeked in her doorway.

"All ready for bed?" Dad asked.

Macie shook her head yes. Here it comes, she thought. If her instincts could be a little more specific, that would be great. *Here comes what?* She briefly wondered if asking yourself questions based off some question that just popped in your head was worse than just plain talking to yourself.

"Mind if we talk for a minute?"

She narrowed one eyebrow, even more curious now about why her dad would want a late night chat after giving her the option of talking earlier. Since she'd told herself to give him a chance, she figured she could start now. At least I had a three second warning, she thought, somewhat confused.

"Your mother used to do that, too. Especially when she couldn't figure out why a person was doing something she didn't understand."

"Do what, Dad?"

"The eyebrow thing. Most people raise an eyebrow. You do it like mom, though and lower one."

Macie pictured her mother's face. Dad was right. She could see Mom making that face.

"You're like her in other ways, too, you know. Do you want to know what happened to me today?" He didn't wait for a response. "I've been getting ready for that big trial on Monday. Today I had a meeting scheduled with one of my key witnesses." He paused a moment. "We were going to review testimony and go over possible questions from the defense team one last time. He hasn't been very cooperative. He's," her dad paused while he thought of something Macie wasn't privy to, then continued, "he's got some problems.

So, I am in my office going through my notes, walking to the places I imagine standing during the beginning and end of his time on the stand. Almost like pacing, I suppose." He'd emphasized the word pacing. He paused again. Macie's eyebrow lowered again. This time it was because she recognized the reference to pacing from her dream. She pushed herself up higher on the bed, leaning her back on her pillow against the headboard.

Her dad continued, "By this time, the guy is half an hour late. I'm looking at the clock and Margie knocks on the door to tell me she just got a call from the station. They arrested him after he failed a urine test. Do you know what that is?"

Now Macie had both eyebrows furrowed. She wasn't sure what it was, but she thought she knew where he was going with this story. She shook her head no and looked straight through his chest.

"That's when they make you pee in a cup to see what's been in your body, like drugs and stuff. What do you think of that, Macie?"

"Are you making fun of me?" Macie's cheeks were red and hot. She felt embarrassed, but she didn't know why.

"Making fun of you? No! No way, Macie." He sat looking at Macie for a moment. "Ahhh, your mother would have been so much better at this. Macie, it all happened. I didn't make it up. And neither did you."

Macie looked thoughtful for a while. She went over Dad's story in her head. She thought back to the dream and Dad's socks this morning.

Macie spoke slowly, "So, you believe I had a dream about you that came true?"

"Pretty much, that's how I see it."

Macie and her dad drifted away into private thoughts. Macie broke the silence first. She was happy that her dad was willing to believe her dreams, but she wasn't sure what to make of it or where he was going with it.

"Lots of people do that, Dad. Don't they? I mean, usually I have them about myself. I've just heard you talking so much that I had a dream about you. I remember Mom always talking to people about her dreams."

"That's why I wanted to talk to you tonight. Because people do dream and I guess sometimes, for whatever reason, it does come true. But most of the time they realize it after the thing has already happened. You thought to tell me first thing this morning, just like Mom would have. She would have told you to pay special attention to your dreams and write them down."

Her dad stopped for a moment. When he continued, he explained, "You know, Mom always kept a dream journal and then if it did actually happen, or even if pieces of a dream happened, she wrote that down when she found out. Then she would compare the dream and how she interpreted it with what really took place. Your mother felt these kinds of dreams are a gift."

Macie waited before she spoke. It was a lot to take in. Then she wondered aloud, "Do you, Dad? Do you think they are a gift? Do you dream like that?"

"Only twice in my life have I remembered a dream that came true. Maybe there have been more and I just didn't notice them or remember them. I think that is what really makes it a gift—that some people can recall in such detail what they see when they sleep. Your mother showed me how useful dreams can be. But, sometimes she had to really work on me to convince me to listen. She always said that I think more in black and white with logic and proof. Your mother trusted her instincts and was usually right. She was gifted in a lot of ways."

"Yeah, but mom was so special. She understood things that no one else seemed to get."

"You're right, Macie. Mom was more special than you even realize yet. She always told me you would be, too. And you know what, squirt? She was so right. In so many ways."

Macie hugged her dad. It was the best, most real hug they'd had in a long time. It was great that for the first time since Mom died they had talked about her without getting sad.

"So, I'm not weird, then?"

"Nope. Just a little more advanced in your dreams than a lot of people."

"I love you, daddy."

"I love you, Macie. If you . . ." he started to say something. Then his tone changed and he teased her, "If you don't get to sleep kiddo, you won't have any time to dream. Kisses and hugs?"

Macie flung open her arms and noticed that they could look into each other's eyes again. They said goodnight. As Macie reached over to turn off the light by her bed, a thought occurred to her.

"Daddy? Gran doesn't like dreams, does she?"

He stopped and turned to look at Macie. "Not really, but why do you ask that?"

"I don't know. I guess it's just a feeling. Maybe it's because she acted funny this morning about your socks. And she gets irritated when I do things like answer the phone before anyone hears it ring. I always thought it was because she was . . . well, old and didn't hear as well as I do. But then James asked how I do that and I know he hears everything."

"Your mother did stuff like that, too."

"Did Gran know that about mom? Why does she act funny about it, then?"

"Hmmm, it's probably too late tonight to explain. And, maybe Aunt Julie would be better able to tell you about it. You'll find that she has more experience in that department than I do. 'K, kiddo?"

"Okay, dad. Can I ask her about it this weekend?"

"I don't see why you couldn't. I know she'll want to hear about your sock dream. Good night now."

"'Night, Dad," she said as he shut her door halfway. And if it hadn't been such a busy, tiring day she would have thought about their conversation. As it was, she dropped off to sleep almost instantly.

$\mathcal{C}$hapter 9

Macie and James finished their Saturday chores in record time. They were going riding today with Gran to check the fences. Gran also had a list of things she wanted to look after while they were out in the fields. The winter's snowfall had been heavy and brutal at times and there were many things that needed to be cleaned up or repaired. Finally, the cold weather had broken. The smell of spring was in the air and buds were forming on the trees.

They saddled up after Gran gave a very thorough inspection. "You have to watch Charlie. He bloats now. We don't want you ending up saddled sideways on your horse now, do we James?" Gran said this every time they went riding.

James laughed as Gran helped him on Charlie and gave him the reins. Macie watched the two of them as she gave Vanity a carrot. Vanity nuzzled Macie's shoulder in thanks. Macie mounted the mare with ease and waited for Gran to mount her steed. Racer X, in his prime, had been as fast and graceful as the breeder had said he'd be. He's lived here for the last few years. He was still beautiful and graceful, but he and Gran seemed to be getting slower together.

Gran started them in the open fields around the fence line. They checked for post damage and downed limbs from the recent storms that had been very windy. They headed up the hill toward the woods. Occasionally, they headed away from the fence to check out something else on Gran's list.

Macie loved to ride. If she could, she'd spend hours up here riding Vanity. Somehow, once you were on top of a horse, connected to their pulse, it was difficult to think of any worries. It always seemed magical and peaceful to Macie.

James, however, was like a tour guide on hoofs. As they headed in different directions, he would call out the names they had given the paths during past visits with Gran. "Here's Mopar Alley." He made revving engine noises and then announced, "And the Charger wins again!" as they passed the shell of an old muscle car sitting between two trees. "Turn Back Lane is just up ahead."

Turn Back Lane was called that because Gran said if they were ever lost without her or another adult, they should turn back at that point. "If you get to the blackberry bushes and the single wooden post, don't go any further into the woods," she had warned. She had told them it was too thick to go by horse and too dangerous to go by foot. A few times last summer they had gone in there without James to pick blackberries. Wearing jeans and long-sleeved shirts in eighty degree weather, they filled buckets for pies and blackberry jelly. Gran knew where the old paths were, but they were overgrown to the untrained eye.

Once, they had made it all the way to where the Pisner's property met Gran's farm. Macie had gotten focused on her blackberry hunt and started to wander away from Gran. "You have to be careful, Macie. We wouldn't want you to fall in a hole," Gran had chided. She had explained about mining that had been done on the land in this area a long time ago.

In the middle of the two properties there had once been a barren area where mining had occurred. Strip mining, she called it.

Today, however, they plodded along the edge of Turn Back Lane and followed the edge of the thick woods to the other side of Gran's property. James pointed out Hidden Hollow a few minutes later and Macie had a sense of déjà vu. It was like she had seen this place in more recent times. She knew she hadn't ridden this way for a while now and struggled to recall why it felt like she had.

She was about to give up when a small piece of last night's dream came to her. She hadn't remembered the dream until just now, as it smacked the inside of her forehead. She still couldn't recall what the dream was about, just the picture of the woods from it. Then, the image from the dream was gone and she was staring at the real image in front of her.

"Macie, are you okay back there? Vanity's not giving you any trouble, is she?"

Macie looked up at Gran. She hadn't realized she had stopped the horse. "Uhh. No, Gran. I'm fine. I just thought I saw something."

Macie wondered if the one detail in the dream must have been part of a bigger dream. I must have dreamt about the woods because I knew we were coming out here today, she surmised. She started Vanity along the trail again as she questioned herself. I wonder why I only remember being right here, though? It's a really weird thing to dream about. I wonder what could have happened in the rest of the dream.

Gran was on the move again, so there was no more time to examine why she was stuck on this dream. Write it down just like Dad said, she told herself.

James started a chant of "what time is it" every two minutes. At least, that's how Gran put it.

"It's two minutes past the last time you asked."

Macie looked over at Gran and smiled while she rolled her eyes. "So, it's two minutes before the next time he asks?" she joked.

"That sounds about right," Gran smiled back, giving her head a little sideways shake.

James was excited about his sleepover with Cousin Andy. It didn't take long to figure out that he wasn't going to let them get any more work done. The trio took a fun route home, giving the horses their heads, allowing them to lead the familiar way home. The kept it slow enough for James. Racer X and Vanity could have galloped, but they instinctively knew to follow Charlie.

When they reached the stable, James was sent off to the house to wash up and relax in his room. Or, at least that's what Gran had told him to do. Dad came out to help take care of the horses. Gran went to the house to make sure James really washed. She and Macie were both sure he wouldn't be relaxing, as excited as he was to play with Andy.

Macie and her dad finished the horses without much talk. Each was lost in their thoughts. Her dad was thinking about his trial and Macie pondered the importance of dreams. What was it Mom used to say? Macie struggled to recall hearing it in her mother's voice. It was getting a little harder as the weeks and months went by. She concentrated, focusing on her mother's image and heard her. 'Dreams are the portal . . .' She almost remembered and concentrated again. 'Dreams are the portal between the past and the present. They are the link between things that have happened and things yet to come." She'd said more, but Macie had a hard time understanding it when it was said. It made it that much more difficult to remember.

Mom's sayings had always seemed too smart to Macie. The words began to play in her mind. She remembered her mother saying that dreams were 'like an opened gate to unlock things you aren't clear about and to help you understand the things you feel to be true.'

Now, what I do with that, she wondered. Hmm. Maybe I should try to dream about my writing assignment and unlock the secret of how to get an A.

"All done, kiddo?" Dad asked, interrupting her thoughts. "Are you ready to go up?"

Macie jumped a little as she heard her dad. She shook her head, no, in response. She wasn't quite as fast or thorough as her dad. He helped her finish up and then they walked across the yard to the house. They were starving and made a mad dash for the kitchen, laughing as they pretended to knock each other out of the way.

Chapter 10

Gran had anticipated their hunger. Lunch was already set on the yellow, daisy placemats. Homemade stew that had simmered all morning and fresh-baked bread out of the oven with butter melting and home-made canned jam on the side waited for them.

"James is packed and ready to go. He can't wait much longer, so I'll run him to Aunt Julie's soon. I have some errands to do in town. Macie, do you want to go?"

"I'm sorry, Gran. I can't. I have to start my writing assignment and finish my math homework today so I can go with Aunt Julie tomorrow. I promised I wouldn't leave it."

Twenty minutes later that's where Macie found herself. She was sitting on her bed, math paper almost done and the English paper looming to the left of her. Normally, she would have been excited to write, but after the last assignment she felt shaky about it. Plus, thinking about her perfect day—the topic for this paper—made her cringe. She couldn't even picture what a good day might be anymore and Mrs. Rich wanted a perfect one?

Riding the horse and working with Gran must have been more tiring than she thought. The fact that she didn't want to write the paper, didn't help. Without even noticing what she was doing Macie leaned back and rested her head on the pillow. She fell into a deep sleep that blocked out all traces of the afternoon sun.

Macie's dream self returned to the spot on Turnback Lane. It seemed dim. Her mind recognized that the sun was setting and that dark was almost upon her.

"Macie!"

Someone in the distance was shouting her name. A small, high-pitched voice called out to her.

"Macie!"

Over and over again, Macie heard her name.

"Macie! Macie . . ."

She sounds scared, her dreaming mind thought. The voice sounds so far away. Then, out of nowhere, a beam of sunlight—the last one of the day—lit a path in front of her.

Macie could see through the brambles into the deepest part of the forest. In her dream, she followed the path carefully and even though she couldn't remember ever being here, Macie could see every detail of the woods. She watched herself stop, waiting.

Waiting for what? Why am I here? The sun was almost gone. Then she heard it again; that small voice calling out to her.

"Macie? Macie, dear. Time for dinner."

Macie recognized the deep timbre of her dad's voice. Suddenly, it registered that she was being called for real.

"Huh?" Her half-aware mind was slowly coming out of its slumber.

"You fell asleep. The fresh air today must have gotten to you. Or did Gran worked you too hard?" he asked, smiling. "Did you get much homework done?"

"My math is done. I still have to write a paper for English, but I'll get it done, too.'

"How about we do our work together tonight? After dinner, we'll set up shop in the living room."

"Okay, dad. I'll be down soon. I just have a couple of other things to write, first."

He looked at her closely, studying her for a moment. He warned her, "Dinner is in ten minutes, kiddo." He winked at her before he shut her door.

Macie looked for a new notebook. She was going to take Dad's suggestion and journal her dreams. She searched her bookshelves and there it was. On the second shelf were the new notebooks that Mom had picked out ages ago. Probably from right around the time she got sick. Mom had given them to her on their last Christmas together.

There, in the middle of the stack was the perfect one with a star pattern on the front. Swirling letters rose and dipped in curves, spelling out the phrase "Believe in Your Dreams" in bright blue letters.

"Thanks, Mom," Macie whispered. "How did you know?"

She hurried to scrawl her dream into the book. She wrote the action first, describing where she started in the dream. Then she put what she saw and where she went in order, writing as many details as she could remember.

She wrote about how the setting sun broke through the trees, cutting ribbons of light on the ground. She had a hard time finding words to show how the trees and bushes looked as she remembered exactly where she had stopped. Sometimes she scribbled a little drawing next to the description.

A large, rectangular boulder jutted up from the dirt on her left. It had a grooved cut in it that gave the stone a layered look. Her dream-self had thought how it was like a bench she could sit upon. To her right was a crabapple tree with its winding branches that looked like claws.

That was as much as she could recall and that was where she finished journaling. It was time to go down for dinner. She paused and wrote one last sentence.

The voice is past the boulder, but it still sounds far away.

Chapter 11

Dinner without James there to chatter on was quiet and uneventful. Gran made it back just before Dad finished steaks on the grill. Macie made a salad and helped Dad cook baked sweet potatoes. Gran and Dad talked a bit about the plans for next week. He'd be leaving early and coming home late. Gran would be working on overtime at home and Macie and James would be expected to pitch in more than usual.

These kinds of weeks were the worst. Gran was great, but Macie missed Mom even more when Dad was gone like this. Mom had always made special plans with James and Macie when Dad had a big case. Once, she had taken them down into her studio and put up easels for them to paint with water colors. She had even allowed them to use her good brushes. She'd spent the afternoon teaching them tricks with shading and lines once they'd finished their paintings. She helped them turn their artwork into something special.

James had started out putting dots all over the canvas. Macie had thought he was messing around, but when Mom checked on him she said it was amazing. He had connected all of the brush taps to make a very real life-like image of their house. It was complete with what appeared to be him, Mom, and Macie waiting on the front porch. A shadowy form of their dad in his dark suit was on the cobblestone path with his back to the viewer.

Mom had been so proud of James. You could see the way her eyes lit up as she told him the good things about his painting. Macie had been extremely jealous. She had gone back to her canvas, pretending to paint more, just so Mom wouldn't see her cry. She looked at her long, broad strokes. Rainbows, balloons, clouds and the sun were spaced around her canvas. It was fun and she had been proud of it until she saw what James had done with his. He had only been four years old.

At some point, Mom had come over to stand behind her. She wrapped her hands around Macie and kissed the top of her head. Macie wiped a tear and her whole body began to shake.

"Macie, honey, what's wrong?" her mother asked.

"Why can't . . . I . . . draw like that? How can James do that? He's just a little kid."

"Oh, Mary Grace, everyone has different talents. You and James have very different, but equally special abilities. You paint pictures with words. When you tell a story, I can picture everything that happened in my mind. I'll bet you could take James' picture and write a wonderful story about it.'

Macie's mom always had a way of making her feel so good about herself.

"Macie, you can't spend your life worrying about what everyone else can do. You be the best that you can be and develop your own talents. The world would be boring if we all had the same skills. What would we look at? What would there be to enjoy if we didn't give each other unique views of the world?"

Macie's mom spent time showing her and James how to add lines and shadows into the pictures that they painted. In the end, they both had paintings that made them very proud.

Macie hadn't thought about that day in a long time. Tonight, though she had an essay to work on. As promised, her dad had set them up in the living room. His briefcase, clipboard, legal pads, pens, and digital recorder sat atop his rolling desk. Macie's erasable pen, notebook and assignment paper were on the coffee table. She curled up in the corner of the couch. Dad was angled toward her from the other corner of the couch.

As her dad got down to business, Macie read over her checklist for the seventeenth time. At the top of the page was the directive, <u>Describe Your Perfect Day</u>. If it hadn't been for Mrs. Rich's advice to talk about things that were real, Macie would have described her perfect day as one spent entirely with her mother. She was avoiding the assignment a little because of that reason. To Macie, there might never be another perfect day. She'd had a couple of good days and better days might be waiting in the wings; maybe even a great day here or there. Perfect seemed to be too far away in her life.

In a perfect day, she thought, Mom would wake me up and I'd be at my old school with all of my friends. Suddenly she perked up. That's it! My perfect day would be to have friends to talk to and hang out with.

Macie wrote about a day that started with picking an outfit that she and her best friend would both have. When she got off the bus, there would always be someone who wanted to sit with her. At school, there were friends waiting for her to join them. They would talk about home and school and boys, and maybe even some really important stuff. There would be notes to pass and seats saved at lunchtime. When she had a bad day, her best friend would be there for her. They would talk with each other on the phone and hang out on the weekends.

Macie wrote two pages for the title, The Perfect Day. The draft, along with ideas for pictures and the page of descriptions that would by typed into the picture captions were complete. Then she checked the assignment sheet to make sure she had included everything expected in the paper. She checked them off the list.

"Who? Me.

What? Friends.

Where? School and home.

When? Well, now, I guess. Wait. Did I put that in there?" She changed the beginning of one sentence to start with the word today.

"Okay, how do I answer why?" She wrote a few lines and ended the assignment with the sentence: Having friends would make me feel happy and maybe I wouldn't miss my mom and my BMD life so much.

Macie finished correcting her paper for indentations, capital letters, paragraph form and spelling. She made a few more notes for the kinds of pictures she wanted to include in computer lab. When she was satisfied, she placed it in her folder and put her things in her book bag.

She went to the kitchen to get a snack. She looked at the clock and couldn't believe how late it was. She passed Gran in the hallway.

"I'm going up to take a bath, Gran." She gave her a quick hug.

"Very good, then. Make sure you wash your hair. Is your dad still working?"

"Yes. He's still in the living room." She headed up the stairs, dragging her bag behind her. She couldn't help but think to herself, I'm not in kindergarten. Of course I won't forget to wash my hair.

By the time she finished her bath and got dressed for bed, her dad was done, too. He asked Macie and Gran if they wanted to play a game before bedtime. They all decided Scrabble would take too long, so they chose between the games of Would You Rather? and Clue. In the end they played Clue and Gran won, guessing Professor Plum in the Conservatory with the wrench.

Macie kissed and hugged Gran and then Dad. He ruffled her hair.

"Is your paper all done?"

"Yes," she answered. "Are you ready for your trial?"

"As ready as I'll ever be. Are you ready for bed?"

She nodded yes. "As ready as I'll ever be," she mimicked.

"Off to bed with you then. Good night."

"Good night, Dad. Love you."

"Love you, too, pumpkin."

Macie slept fitfully that night. Images of dark rooms and dirt, then shadows and trickling water randomly popped through her dreams.

"Macie."

The voice called for her again. It sounded familiar this time.

Chapter 12

Macie's Sunday began as usual. Get up. Get ready for church in a hurry. Cause Gran to get nervous about being late. Race out the door. Wait for Gran in the car since she was always last anyway. Pray a little.

After church, they ate brunch at a local restaurant. When they returned home, there were chores to do. Macie had to put away her clean laundry, peel potatoes for Gran's potatoes au gratin and water the horses. She finished with record speed, thinking the whole time about the day ahead with Aunt Julie.

She was changing her clothes for the third time that day when she heard Aunt Julie's car pull up the drive. As she was gathering her rarely used purse and her shoes, James raced up the porch steps and bounded through the door. Before he could even catch his breath he shouted.

"That was the best sleepover, ever!" Then he recited a scattered chain of events that he and cousin Andrew shared at Aunt Julie's house. "We played the Wii and I beat Andrew at Hot Wheels. Uncle Steve played 6 games of Go Fish! with us and then took us fishing at the river. We got to make our own pizzas for dinner last night and we saw a . . ." Macie, having heard none of this, was halfway through the door with James still babbling away.

She ran to Aunt Julie and threw her arms around her.

"Hi, Aunt Julie!"

"Hi, there!" she laughed as she greeted the enthusiastic Macie. "Are you ready to go?"

"I sure am. I've been ready since the day you called."

Aunt Julie laughed again and then they said their goodbyes to Gran, James, and her dad. Dad told Macie to let Aunt Julie help her pick out some new school outfits. Macie's dad had no sense of girl fashion or the patience to wait while she figured it out on her own. When Aunt Julie was able to help her, Macie was always thrilled. Dad and Gran still wanted to dress her like she was in first grade. Ugh!

The mall was twenty minutes away. They talked about James and Andrew. Macie chatted about riding horses with Gran. She almost told Aunt Julie about the spot in the woods but it made her feel weird, so she didn't. A song they both liked played on the radio and they sang together, laughing when they stumbled over the words they didn't remember.

The mall was busy this Sunday afternoon. The buttery smell of warm, soft pretzels filled the air. The artful window displays showed the latest fashion in all of the trendiest colors. Sapphire blue and canary yellow seemed to be everywhere. Aunt Julie commented that she had never really felt that she could wear yellow clothes. Macie spied a fluorescent green top.

"Now there's a color I wouldn't dare try on," Macie said as she made a funny face.

And, that was that. They had to go into that store and try on all the craziest colors. It turned out that the green shirt looked really cool with the pair of black leggings that had a green flower—fluorescent, of course—stitched on the calf.

They made it through three more stores before they got hungry. The pair made their way to the food court, giggling about some of the disastrous outfits they'd seen. Macie was happy that she found several really nice outfits. Aunt Julie knew how to bargain shop with style. She had also shown Macie how to mix and match several of the items so that she could create new looks out of the same clothes.

They split up to order food from two places. Aunt Julie headed to the Chinese counter and Macie went to the fish-n-chips place. When they met back in the middle and found a table, they halved their orders and shared them with one another.

"This is so good," Aunt Julie said as she picked at another piece of orange chicken.

"I know. Homemade food is nice, but nothing beats Chinese," Macie said.

They ate until every bite was gone. Even the large drinks were drained. They both said they were full and would never eat again until they passed the ice cream shop on the way out of the food court. They bought two ice cream cones dipped in chocolate that had hardened and headed out into the crowds again. Macie thought the mall was so pretty. Everything sparkled. The smell of newness was refreshing.

The shoe store caught their eye and they couldn't resist. They looked at one another and without saying a word, immediately walked to the storefront. New shoes were like a magnet. They drew your feet to them with such force that you could not help but to walk into them.

Aunt Julie and Macie headed to the women's section. Macie had long left the girls sizes with her size six feet. Some shoes they laughed over. Some, they bragged about and strutted their catwalk abilities. Macie found a great pair of brown boots that she adored. One time, they even pulled the same shoe, in their respective sizes, off the shelves.

"I love these!" Macie and Aunt Julie shouted at the same time. They tried on the pair of brown, leather clogs. They went to the register next, both deciding the clogs were the perfect shoe.

Macie noticed a shoe display in the front window and got very quiet. Aunt Julie paid for their purchases. As they walked toward the exit, Macie lingered at the display. She rubbed one finger over the silky texture.

"Mom would have loved this shade of purple."

Aunt Julie hesitated for just a moment. She put her hand on Macie's shoulder and looking right at the jewel-studded ballet flat, she agreed.

"Oh, yes! She sure would have, Macie." As she saw Macie's face tighten and an eye glisten with the beginning of a single tear, she pulled her into a one-arm bear hug and guided her out of the mall. They walked down the rows of cars, leaning on one another.

"I miss her too, honey. A lot."

$\mathcal{C}$hapter 13

Macie didn't speak; couldn't speak, until they got to the car. She was certain she would choke on her unshed tears. She slid into the front seat while Aunt Julie opened the trunk and put their bags inside. She separated her packages from Macie's so they would find them easily when she they got back to Macie's house. She also did this to give Macie a little time. By the time Aunt Julie got into the car, Macie felt that she had herself under control.

That was true until Aunt Julie looked over at her and using one of her endearing terms for Macie, asking, "You okay, mia chica?"

NO! She screamed inside her head. Macie's lip trembled. Then out of nowhere she exploded with an outpouring of emotion.

"I hate this!"

After she opened the floodgate there was no stopping her.

"I hate that mom left me. That she isn't here to take me to the mall; to buy ice cream together; to try on shoes." She hesitated briefly and then said quietly, "I loved being with you today, Aunt Julie, but the whole day I kept missing mom." Her voice rose again. "It isn't fair! That stupid shoe—I saw it and thought of mom. It just looked like a shoe to have fun in. Just like how fun Mom always was. I miss having fun with her! I miss having fun at all. Nothing . . . Nothing seems the same without her. The sky isn't as blue. Playing isn't as happy. It's like when she died, she took all the good stuff with her."

Macie drew a deep breath and continued, "I miss our house. I miss her voice, her laugh, the way she smelled. And it's awful that I don't have anyone to talk to about the big stuff. She always made me feel better and I want her back. I want to talk about the dreams I have and dad and school stuff. And, and . . . It's just not fair!" Macie ended her tirade loudly.

Aunt Julie sat silently, biting her tongue. She felt awkward and didn't want to just say some off-handed thing. She hated it when other people did that to her, but she wasn't sure where to begin. Instead of talking, she scooted over to the middle of the seat and opened her arms. She pulled Macie to her and wrapped her arms around her. They both sat there crying for a few minutes. Macie shook from the intensity of her feelings. Aunt Julie moved only once, to grab tissues from the glove compartment.

After a while the tears subsided and their breaths returned to normal. They straightened up and leaned back into the seat, pushing their feet onto the dash so that their knees were bent.

"I think that's what I miss the most, too, Macie—having someone to talk with. Your mom and I talked about everything. Now, when I want to share something important or sad or funny with someone, I feel lost because she's gone. Sometimes, I'll even forget and I'll try to pick up the phone and call her. Then I'll remember she's gone and I feel so let down."

"Me, too. I've turned to call her name and then feel stupid for forgetting she's gone. I'll want to talk about my stories or a dream that I've had. She's not here to help me, so I don't know what to do."

"You know, your mom and I used to talk about dreams all the time." Aunt Julie waited, looking thoughtful and because it seemed right to share, carefully said, "We even had some dreams that we felt came true."

Macie's head perked up. Finally! Someone who might truly understand her. Not just believe her, but really get it. She told Aunt Julie the sock dream she had about Dad. With a little encouragement from her aunt, Macie didn't feel so crazy anymore.

"Some dreams feel so right that you just know it's telling you something. Or it feels real in the dream because it has the potential to be real," Aunt Julie explained.

Macie bit her bottom lip and lowered her one eyebrow. She was concentrating on the details of her latest dream. As she pictured it, she started to describe the woods and the déjà vu feeling to Aunt Julie that she'd had when riding with Gran. She got a prickly feeling on the back of her neck as she spoke.

"I feel like there is more to the dream, but I am afraid to see what's going to happen next. I can still hear that voice calling my name. It sounds so familiar. It makes me afraid to see what comes next though, because it feels like it could be a nightmare. Everything about it feels scary. It's so strange that it can't possibly be something that will come true, but could it be trying to tell me something?"

Aunt Julie paused, thinking. "Well, you could pray before you go to sleep. Pray that if you need to have this dream and there's something you need to know from it, that God will help you and protect you. If it's something bad or scary, tell yourself its ok to let yourself wake up."

"Well, I guess I can . . . try that. You mean God helps with dreams?"

"I think God, in whatever form he is in, is always with us and wants us to be safe. I think we are all part of the universe and are connected to each other by something."

"I'm not sure I understand that, but I'll give that prayer thing a try."

Aunt Julie nodded and moved back to the driver's seat. "Macie, I promised your mom I would be here for you and help you with the things that your dad just won't be any good with. This is one of those things. If you ever need to talk about something, you can always call me. If you need help with anything, I will be here. And whenever you have a dream you want to share, I can try to figure it out with you."

"I love you, Aunt Julie. Thanks."

"I love you, too, Macie."

They spent the ride home talking about Macie's old school and her new school and how hard it was to fit in and make new friends. They shared more about Macie's mom and how much she had felt that dreams really guided her choices. By the time they pulled into Gran's driveway, Aunt Julie promised to have Macie come over to her house for a sleepover in a few weekends. She told Macie they could call one or two of her old friends to come over when she did. Macie felt better than she had in weeks, but was exhausted. All of that crying and I-miss-Mom talk had wiped her out.

Chapter 14

It took Macie exactly three minutes from the time she entered the house until she was dropping bags into her bedroom. She looked at the bags of new clothes and considered sorting and organizing them just so she could see them again. As much as she wanted to do just that, she left everything in the bags piled at the bottom of her bed. She lay down on the bed filling the spot above the clothes.

Macie went face first into her pillow thinking that a little nap would be very nice. As she drifted off to sleep she heard Aunt Julie's voice in the back of her mind.

Macie quietly asked, "If I am supposed to dream, please guide me and protect me." She added in a soft voice, "Let me wake up if I get too scared of the dream, but help me to be brave."

She was so tired that she fell asleep in less than ten seconds. It was like the dream had been bookmarked. It started where it had last ended. Standing again beside the bench-like boulder, her dream-self looked over the area again. The gray bark of the crab apple tree blended into the dusky night. Those last embers of sunlight were fading and darkness was slipping over the horizon.

A picture flashed before her like a dream within a dream. Bushes and vine-covered paths were leading to the top of a trophy with a dancer at its top. The metal statue was crying and then the sky went black.

Macie edged carefully through the forest, feeling the need to watch her feet. She followed the path as if a magnet pulled her to itself. Her mind ticked a mental count of her steps that she didn't hear until she got close to the goal she'd been shown.

The trophy rose in front of her. There was no need to go any further. Remember this, she thought. This is the spot. The spot for what, she wondered to her dream keepers. And then, the statue spoke to her.

"I'm here Macie. Right here. Please find me." This time the voice was crystal clear and loud.

Macie woke slowly, recalling the details of her dream. She was out of bed and reaching for her notebook before she was fully aware of what she was doing. She needed to get that spot down on paper. She wrote: two-hundred sixty-seven steps from the boulder to the dancing trophy. That is where the voice is at its loudest.

"Grrr! It makes no sense. Why can't it just be simple?" Macie questioned her dream in frustration. She kept writing.

She worked her way back from the place around the trophy to the beginning at the boulder. She continued writing as fast as she could, leaving out no details.

She thought as she wrote. But, why would the trophy ask me to find it when I'd already found it?

Macie headed downstairs, feeling more than confused. It's just weird, she thought. If this dream is supposed to mean something, why can't I see something that makes sense? A stupid dancer trophy is sitting in the middle of the woods. What's next, she asked herself? Her sarcastic response followed. Alice is going to fall down the rabbit hole into

Wonderland? She smacked her forehead with the palm of her hand. It doesn't mean anything to me and it probably isn't supposed to anyway, she thought in frustration.

Macie decided the dream must have more to show her, if was even supposed to mean anything. She headed downstairs. Whenever she ate Chinese, she always felt hungry within a couple of hours. Still irritated, she yanked open the refrigerator door and pulled out the ice tea pitcher. She walked to the counter and started pouring a glass of tea and noticed her name written at the top of a note on the counter.

The note, in her dad's scrawling handwriting read:

Macie,

I got called in to help with a situation for work. I'm not very far away, so if you need me, just call. There's a missing girl from your school and we are all out looking for her. Don't be afraid if you hear it on the news. We will find her.

Love,

Dad

Thankfully, Macie had already set the pitcher on the counter. The color had faded from her face and her arms and legs felt about as strong as Gran's jelly. She was rooted in her spot while her mind worked overtime.

Suddenly the nonsense dream flashed in front of her eyes.

"That's it! I know what the dream meant. Someone is calling out to me and I can help Dad find them." Macie realized. She felt elated and sick at the same time.

Her mind raced. How could the dream be real in that way, though? Horribly and terribly real. Macie shook her head from side to side as if to fling the understanding away. It can't be. If I'm right, someone is lost and scared and alone and waiting for me to find them. The voice in the woods haunted her thoughts. It's most definitely a girl's voice, she told herself. I have to find her. And then Macie felt so weak that she almost fainted. She needed to sit, but the chair was so far away that she just slid down the cabinets and sat on the floor.

The single word, "No," slipped from her lips.

Macie shook her head. It just couldn't be what she was thinking. She went over the dream and the sound of the voice and put it together with the little bit of information from her dad's note. She was sure.

"It's Annie," she whispered. A cold chill fanned out over her body. Annie Carter is calling out to me, Macie thought as the voice echoed in her mind.

She could be hurt and I need to find her. No one is going to believe me if I tell them that I know where she is. Even if they do, will they think I am crazy? How can I explain how I know where she is?

Macie couldn't breathe, could not think; could not act. She sat.

Then a calm settled over her and she focused on what the dream wanted her to do. "It doesn't matter. I have to help. I have to get to Dad. He'll know what to do about this."

In a split second, she was up off of the floor. She grabbed the phone and raced up the stairs. She flung open the drawers, searching for her hiking clothes. She used the time it took to change to go over her dream, trying to remember more details. It also gave her a chance to think of how to tell Dad.

Before she could find all the reasons not to, she dialed her dad's cell number. First ring. She waited. Second ring. It felt like forever.

"Come on. Answer," Macie said into the receiver.

Third ring. Heart racing, stomach sinking. Halfway through the fourth ring, Macie finally heard her dad's voice.

"Gran?"

"Dad!" They spoke at the same time.

"Oh, Macie, honey . . . I . . . I'm busy right now. I really can't talk . . . . Is everything?"

Macie didn't give him the chance to finish asking if everything was okay at home.

"Dad, I know. I know you're busy. I read your note. Dad, I had a . . . Well, I can help you. I can find the girl. I know where she is." She avoided saying she knew who she was.

"Macie, honey, all anyone knows is that this little girl was visiting her grandparent's farm and no one has seen her since yesterday."

"That's just it, Dad. Listen to me, please! I know where she is. I know where to find her."

"Macie, how could you know that?'

"I had a dream."

She waited.

And, waited.

Then she could almost hear her dad groan. "A dream? Macie, I cannot tell everyone here to go searching based on something you saw in a dream. I just . . . can't. Don't worry. We are looking everywhere and asking neighbors."

"No! Arrrhh! I know it's from a dream, but I also know she's in trouble. I think she must be covered up somehow because I can't hear her voice very well. I have it written in my journal. She's lonely and scared. It will be dark soon and she's right here on Turnback Alley. We have to go and get her."

Nothing happened. Macie hadn't been sure what to expect, but she didn't think her dad wouldn't say anything.

"Daddy? Daddy, please just come home. Come get me. I'm right. I know I am."

And again, nothing but voices in the background on her dad's end. She was done waiting for a response.

"Fine, dad. Don't believe me. Forget the dream about your socks; forget any of that. The Pisner's must be her grandparents, right? I'll go find Annie myself." She hung up the phone without hearing him ask her where she thought the missing girl was.

The click of the connection ending was like a timer being started. She was going to be in so much trouble for so many things by bedtime that she started a mental list.

Hanging up on Dad will be the least of it, Macie thought as she grabbed her backpack and some supplies. Let's see. Taking out the horse without an adult; going past Turn Back Alley; being out alone after dark; acting on crazy dreams. I'll be grounded for life.

I'd better get going.

Chapter 15

The fear of being in trouble did not sway her from her mission. She had grabbed the backpack and sprinted to the stable. Somehow she had found herself more adept at saddling up than she ever had before. Her nerves, alert and aware, signaled her muscles to act from memory. As she swung up onto the freshly saddled mare, Macie began to calm down.

"At least if I'm wrong, I won't have to look stupid in front of a million people. It's just you and me, Vanity."

The horse never broke out of a trot. Macie wanted to hurry, but she also wanted to be safe. It gave her time to think over the things she had put in the backpack between the house and the stable. The journal with her directions was tucked in with several other items. She had rope, a blanket, some bottled water, the small first aid kits, a flare, and a utility knife. Most things had been in the hall closet. The last two items, found on a shelf in the stable, would add to her grounding, but she felt they might be necessary.

She wasn't sure how useful any of that would be in the end, but it had made her feel prepared. She was prepared, but without a plan. It was like searching for a treasure. She had the map but wasn't sure if her tools would get her through the "X" on the spot when she found it. In her case, a trophy marked the spot. Maybe.

"Too late to worry now," Macie said to Vanity as they came up on Turnback Alley.

"Whoa, girl," she said as she slowed the horse to a halt. She lowered herself to the ground while she praised her horse. Walking to the front of the beloved mare, she patted and rubbed Vanity gently before looping the reins around the wooden post that sat alone at the edge of the woods.

"I wish I had remembered the carrots, girl. Be good, now. I'll be back soon. I hope."

Macie pulled her journal and a flashlight out of her backpack while thinking, I guess this is 'do or die' time. Then she shivered at the thought. Crossing the path through the blackberry bushes felt like entering another world. Macie had only been through these woods with Gran when the sun was high in the sky. Now the sun was setting and the tree canopy made it seem like night had already come.

The images from her dream were all here. She could not hear anything yet and she was so afraid that her throat locked and would not let her call out. She walked toward the only bit of sun that hit the ground and prayed her dream was sending her in the right direction.

Jaggers and briars pulled against her jeans as if they were sticky hands grabbing at her. She worked her body around and away from them.

And then, she just stopped and started talking to herself.

"This is crazy. Even if I find anything, it will be too dark to find my way back. The sun is almost gone. Even Hansel and Gretel were smart enough to leave a trail of bread crumbs behind them. If I get myself lost too, dad's going to have my head."

She finished the next thought in silence. This is it, though. I know I'm right.

She sat down on the boulder from her dream. She ran her hand over the hard, cool top. The rough texture of the stone let Macie know this was all very real. Something inside her told her to stop and wait right there. Minutes ticked by as Macie stared at the crabapple tree while it faded to gray and began to disappear against the darkness. She couldn't go back, but she couldn't go forward.

"Why?" She begged her mind to answer.

The answer came so suddenly that she jumped into mid-air and let out a screech. From one side a small voice cried out to her. But, from the other side she could hear the sound of an ATV motor and someone loudly calling her name over the rumble of the engine.

The ATV slowed and quieted to a puttering hum. The engine cut off and Macie thought she heard Vanity snort her displeasure, but might have imagined it.

When she heard her name again, she recognized Aunt Julie's voice instantly. "Macie! Are you here?"

Relief washed over her. "Aunt Julie, I'm here. Can you hear me?"

"Yes, honey. I hear you. Where are you? I'm coming. Your dad's on his way."

She felt a jolt of panic knowing that her dad was coming. Aunt Julie could help smooth things over with him. Hopefully.

"In the woods. Umm . . . let's see. Go to the left of Vanity. Over where the bushes are. There are two that make a little opening. That's where I started." Macie yelled into the forest, trying to guide her aunt to her place at the boulder.

Macie waited a minute and then Aunt Julie asked, "Okay, Macie. Now, where?"

"Start looking to your right for another opening. You shouldn't have to walk too long before you find it."

Macie heard it again. Stronger this time, the other voice cried out to her.

"Hurry, Aunt Julie. Someone needs help. I can hear her. Did you find the opening?"

"Yes, Macie. I found it. I'm coming."

"Just keep walking where it is mostly open. There are a lot of blackberry bushes to get caught on." Macie rubbed at her hand where she had the scratches to prove that fact.

"Just keep talking, Macie. I'm following your voice. How did you end up in here?"

Macie told her how she fell asleep once she was home and filled in the details of how her dream had finished. She replayed the conversation with her dad and how she broke all the rules to follow this dream. She had gotten to the part about knowing she'd be grounded for months and not caring anymore when she saw Aunt Julie's head, outlined in the light of a lantern, bobbing above the bushes bringing her to the spot where Macie now stood.

As her aunt followed the path Macie had just taken, Macie told her, "I've been sitting here waiting to walk the last steps. I didn't know why and then I heard you coming. I guess I was supposed to wait for you." Aunt Julie crossed the last few steps to Macie.

They gave each other a huge hug. Aunt Julie looked at Macie and said, "We should wait for your dad to get here. He called me when you wouldn't answer his return calls to see if I was close enough to double back. You didn't give him the chance to ask where she is."

Macie felt a little relief, knowing that dad had been going to trust her. Trepidation crept in when she wondered if he would be upset that she had bolted with the facts of her dream guiding her. Remembering the dream and why she was getting damp in the woods, she begged her aunt, "Please, can't we just go a little farther? We're so close."

Aunt Julie had already known she wouldn't be able to wait for Macie's dad. She had specifically made sure she didn't promise that outright. She wanted to know just as badly as Macie did. "Where do we go from here?"

"It's straight ahead. Macie felt too silly to be specific about the number of steps she took in her dream and told her aunt, "It's almost two-hundred and seventy-five steps from here."

Aunt Julie stared at Macie for a moment before asking, "Your dream was really that specific? That's amazing!"

Macie grinned. "It was actually two-hundred sixty-seven steps from this boulder to the . . . the spot I saw in my dream." There was no way she was going to explain that she was looking for a trophy with a dancing figure on top in the middle of the woods. Aunt Julie might be supporting her, but spilling that detail could very well make her just turn around and go home.

"All right. Let's try it, Macie. Just be careful. Keep your flashlight on the ground in front of you."

Macie took the lead while her aunt used her cell to check in with her dad. She told him where to find them. From the conversation on Aunt Julie's end, Macie assumed her dad was not happy that they weren't sitting as still as that boulder and waiting for him.

"Your dad will be here in five minutes. They're at the stable now. I had to promise we'd stop, but a few more feet or so shouldn't hurt anything." She winked at Macie.

Macie stopped so she didn't lose count at number two hundred forty-six. She said the number out loud for Aunt Julie to hear. Then she shouted out to the darkness.

"We're here, if you can hear us. Help is coming. We're here!" Macie shouted out hoping Annie could hear her.

Then to Aunt Julie she said, "What if I can't find her? What if I didn't remember it right and they look in the wrong spot?"

As if to answer, the voice called out again. This time they could hear the word, "help."

"Macie, close your eyes for a minute and try to feel that magnet from your dreams. And, Macie, it's okay. You got us this far. We can hear her. Your dad is coming with help and they can take it from there."

Macie felt the pressure lift. She tried closing her eyes. They were now only about twenty dream-steps away, but there was no gold trophy anywhere in sight. The voice was louder, but not exactly clear. She looked for anything gold.

Macie walked as far as she felt she was supposed to go. When her brain told her feet to stop, she stayed rooted to the ground. It was as if her feet had become cement blocks. But, there was still no sign of anyone. Annie wasn't here. She was nowhere to be seen. It was dark and Macie felt like she had failed. She felt foolish for thinking a gold trophy was going to be in the woods.

Aunt Julie called out, "Hello. Can you hear me? Is anyone here?"

Aunt Julie asked," Macie can you stop and sit down here while I shine my light around?" Macie did as she was asked. Then she decided to try one more time.

"Hello! Annie? Are you here?"

The sound they were looking for finally came as Aunt Julie's light flashed over a sunken part of the ground just a few feet in front of them. It was Annie's voice; Annie called out to them.

"I'm here! Please get me out. Please."

She was under the ground.

From behind them, the pair realized that there were branches and twigs breaking and voices calling out for each of them.

"We're here," her aunt yelled.

"She's here," Macie announced at the same time.

Chapter 16

The stillness of the night broke like the finale of a Fourth of July fireworks display. In one swift moment the steady symphony of crickets was drowned out. The rustle of trees, stomping of boots and screams of excitement created a blur of action. It was as if time stood still and flew by all at once.

Macie's dad ran over to her and hugged her tightly.

"I'm sorry, Macie. I'm so glad you're safe." Others joined her father and surrounded Macie. A few people talked with her aunt.

Macie answered questions without remembering what she heard or spoke. Movement was so chaotic around her. Eventually, she focused her eyes on the dark outline of the forest.

She did not remember leaning into Aunt Julie's arms and drifting off to sleep. She did not dream, but in her sleep, her mother came to sit with her. There was no need to speak as they could hear each other's thoughts.

I'm so proud of you, Macie. It's hard to trust in your feelings or to believe in things that seem to have no explanation. You did just that and you have saved your friend.

Macie could feel the warmth of her mother's hug. She had missed that so much this past year. She would have preferred to stay this way forever, but suddenly the warm circling of her mother's arms was replaced by cold hands.

Instantly she came out of her dream-like state and resisted as someone tried to lift her away from Aunt Julie.

"NO!" she screamed when she heard them say they were taking her home. "No!" she pleaded and the motion stopped.

"I have to stay. I have to know if Annie's okay," Macie explained adamantly.

She waited anxiously to hear the response. Nothing was said, but a moment later she was covered with a heavy, coarse blanket. Aunt Julie stroked her hair as they sat out of the way against the boulder.

The rescue work had moved quickly during Macie's nap. The entire area was flooded with light and some kind of machinery, as well as even more people, had been put into place. A squared-off section of earth about twenty-five feet from the spot Macie had pointed out was a hub of activity. Macie sucked in her breath when she saw it.

"Aunt Julie, they're digging in the wrong spot!" she whispered. "We have to tell them," Macie implored as she grabbed her aunt's arm. Macie's face was strained and her eyes squinted into mere slits as she focused on the workers in the clearing.

Macie's aunt reassured her, "No, Macie. It's fine. They are right where they need to be. They can't dig over top of her or . . ." she let the end of her sentence fade. "Honey, they know what they are doing." She held Macie tightly to keep her from running into the rescue zone.

Macie relaxed her body, but her eyes showed fear and worry. She was confused and disoriented. Her concern for Annie was overwhelming. Her heart pounded fiercely in her chest.

"Macie?" A woman's voice asked softly.

Macie turned her head, surprised at the sound of the unfamiliar voice. She looked up to see a tall woman with short, spiky brown hair. She looked so tired to Macie with her sagging eyes. Macie slowly nodded to the lady.

"Macie, I'm Mrs. Carter. Carol Carter. Annie's mom." She spoke each word in a slow, purposeful way.

Macie could not explain why that introduction made her cry when she heard it. She broke down, sobbing, barely able to breathe. The weight of all her fears and worries poured out in the streams of tears.

Annie's mother took Macie into her arms. At first, Macie shuddered and sobbed as her body shook with all of the emotions of the day.

"It's okay, honey. It's okay now," Mrs. Carter choked out the words between her own tearful hiccups. She assured Macie, "they are working, Macie. She'll be out soon. Annie's going to be out soon."

"Are you sure? Is she . . . Did she get hurt?" Macie had worried so much that Annie had really injured herself. She knew she wouldn't believe she was okay until she saw Annie for herself. "How long has she been down there?"

"Honey, I am as sure as I can be. She went for a walk on my parent's farm yesterday and we couldn't find her at dinner time. Now we think she may have been trying to find your house through the woods. But, we had started looking in the wrong direction, never thinking that she would have gone so far into the woods on her own. She says she needs to talk to you as soon as she is out. She tried to get them to let her talk to you now, but no one is allowed near the rescue zone."

Macie's eyes welled up with salty tears again. This time they felt like a cleansing rain as they fell. Mrs. Carter pulled Macie into her arms again and held her tightly.

It felt good to be held by a mom. Even if it couldn't be her own, right now a mother's touch was exactly what Macie needed. She wobbled a bit and Annie's mom helped her sit again on the blanket.

Carol sat down on the ground at Macie's side. Aunt Julie flanked her other side. The strength of both women gave Macie a deep sense of peace and courage. They quietly watched as the rescue team moved with efficiency and purpose. A large drill-like machine was slowly tunneling into the earth.

"They are going to make a hole large enough to fit a crew member and Annie. Then, they'll tunnel across to get her. They will strap her to the safety harness and lift them both out together," Annie's mom filled them in.

"How far down is she?" Aunt Julie asked, peeking around Macie's head to see Mrs. Carter.

"They sent her down a bottle of water, some crackers, and a flashlight and it was about thirty feet to reach her."

Macie missed the look that passed over her head between the two mothers. At the same time, Aunt Julie and Carol reached for Macie's hands. Macie felt as if an electric spark ran through her body. She wasn't sure why, but it was as if she was able to think and see clearer.

They all watched together as the drill was raised out of the second, larger hole. Macie hadn't realized how noisy it was until it stopped. She watched men and women gathering together, talking and moving their arms. As the group continued their discussion, a man was being fitted into a safety-harness. Two other men checked various points on the harness. A small cocoon-like material with holes for legs was clipped onto the metal rings of the man's harness.

He stood, waiting while Macie sat watching. I wish they would stop talking already so he can go, Macie thought.

Two minutes felt like thirty, but finally the group of talkers dispersed. One woman walked toward the harnessed man. She spoke for several minutes. He nodded a lot but Macie didn't see him speak often. Macie felt as if she would go crazy if that man did not get into the hole soon. Couldn't they have talked this out while they were drilling the hole?

"Oh, come on already!" Mrs. Carter shook her head. "Get my baby out now."

Macie squeezed her hand. "I know. I was just thinking something like that. I want to scream."

Aunt Julie chimed in, "Me, too!"

And with that, the woman nodded and the harnessed man stepped toward the entrance. Above the hole, an electric pulley had been positioned. The ropes from the pulley were attached to the metal loops on the man's safety gear. The man sat at the edge of the hole. He swung around, chest to the ground and the ropes began to lower after he placed his feet against the inside of the hole. In less than ten seconds, he was completely gone.

"Now what do we do?" Macie asked.

"We wait," answered Annie's mom.

"And pray," Aunt Julie added.

Several people came over to them as they sat and watched for any signs. When a miniature version of the drill was lowered into the hole, Macie looked around, confused.

The talking woman who seemed to be in charge answered Macie's unspoken question. "He still has to dig across to reach Annie."

"Oh. Oh . . . I didn't think of that. How long is that going to take?"

"It depends on how rocky the earth is there. We think it is hard enough to stay in place while he drills, but soft enough to get through without breaking the drill. It should take a few minutes per foot, so we estimate at least an hour," Miss Lady-In-Charge said.

Macie had listened but not really heard the explanation. She did catch the one hour wait time. Really? Really, now??? Macie was so beyond all this waiting. She was impatient and so tired that she wondered if she would be awake to see Annie come out. Then she felt guilty for being tired when she thought about all that Annie was going through.

The wait was horrible, but Aunt Julie and Annie's mom made it a little better for Macie. They talked about Mrs. Rich and the girls' class. Out of the blue Macie pondered, "Do I have to go to school in the morning?"

Carol laughed and Aunt Julie made a big scene about checking her watch while she said, "Sunrise is about two hours away. I would think that you are going to get the day off."

"I hope so. Wonder what Gran will say?" Macie must have made a face without realizing it because Carol laughed again and Aunt Julie shook her head.

They didn't get a chance to discuss what Gran would say as the area around the rescue zone suddenly became a beehive of activity. Macie and her aunt stood up quickly to see what was happening. Macie looked over to ask Annie's mother if she thought Annie was on her way out. She realized that Annie's mom was still sitting on the ground and had started to shake. Macie felt the need to be protective. A little voice told her it was almost over and her job was to help Annie's mom get through it.

"Mrs. Carter? Carol? It's okay. She's coming. Annie's almost here. She's going to be fine. I know she is."

Carol nodded her head and stood up. It felt as if the entire planet stopped for a moment. Without any prompt, the people surrounding the zone split like the Red Sea parting. The three of them made their way toward the front. It seemed like they moved in a flash while the rest of the world was moving backwards. The wires of the harness circled around and around as it lifted out of the hole. A slightly audible grating noise stuck in Macie's head as she focused on reaching the goal once again. As they reached the destination, Miss Lady-In-Charge met with them.

"She's on her way, Mrs. Carter. By the rescuer's account it looks as if she is doing well. The ambulance is on standby in the driveway. Someone can take you down on the ATV if you want to go with Annie to the hospital. They are ready for her at Children's as soon as we get her there."

Macie hadn't thought much about what would happen once Annie was out. She hadn't realized they would send her to Pittsburgh instead of one of the local hospitals. Her mind started to wander but was interrupted by shouts and clapping as two heads emerged from the ground. Macie and her aunt hugged and squeezed each other while tears streamed over their faces. Mrs. Carter and Annie's dad had found each other and were locked in an embrace as they overlooked the scene waiting for their daughter to fully appear. Every face in the crowd was lit with joy and relief. A collective euphoria set in as Annie and her rescuer were lowered on top of the ground and Annie was gently placed on a stretcher. Success! Everyone felt it. Everyone was a part of it. The moment was something that those who were experiencing it together would never, ever forget.

Macie moved a little closer and watched as Annie's parents touched her gently, rubbing her head or arm as they whispered words with one another that would be part of their moment. The EMT's had done their job and just by the shift in the way they stood and the focus they gave toward the woods, the crowd understood that it was time to go. Aunt Julie stood behind Macie with her arms wrapped around her as Annie was slowly rolled past them.

Annie and Macie's eyes met and the connection of the night was sealed. Annie asked the EMT to wait and one of them motioned Macie to her. Annie's voice was barely a whisper and Macie had to lean over her to hear.

"Thank you, Macie. I knew you would come when I called. I saw it. I knew you would find me."

Before Macie could respond, Annie was in motion again. Macie stood rooted to the ground.

Apparently her dream wasn't just a one way connection. If Macie was hearing her right, Annie had clicked the send/receive button directly between hers and Macie's brain.

Chapter 17

Macie lay in a deep slumber. As soon as Annie was whisked away from her to the safety of the ambulance waiting in Gran's driveway, her mind had shut down. Her last thought had been one of shock as she realized that Annie had somehow known she was coming to get her. She barely remembered being jostled on the ATV through the woods. She had no memory of being placed in her bed.

She slept.

And she slept.

And then, she may have dreamed again.

Her mother was sitting beside her on the bed.

My little angel has had a very long night, hasn't she? Macie honey, you are going to have to wake up soon. If you keep sleeping, people will be worried. I love you, Mary Grace.

Macie heard her mother's voice and the fog in her brain slowly lifted. She could smell the lilac-scented perfume her mother wore and it surrounded her. She could feel the love her mother sent as she awakened to a bright sun-filled afternoon.

She allowed herself to treasure the moment and pocket it as a new memory with her mom.

"You're still here, aren't you mom? I feel you. Stay with me."

"What time is it?" Macie moaned as she rolled over to see her clock. Her eyes widened when she saw it was after two o'clock. She wasn't sure how long she had been asleep and felt disoriented from waking in the afternoon.

She stayed in bed thinking about the hours before she slept. As the questions started to invade her mind, she became completely alert.

How's Annie?

Where's Annie?

How did she know I could find her?

How much trouble am I in?

Who's here right now?

What's Gran going to say?

The last question was one she wanted to avoid for a while. She had meant to ask Aunt Julie why Gran was always so sullen whenever dreams or anything unusual was mentioned, but had forgotten both times she was with her aunt.

She still didn't understand why, but she knew Gran would not be happy about the latest development on the dream front. She could feel it. She wasn't sure she was going to like the answer, either. Feeling a little anxious, Macie headed to the bathroom peeking through the hallway to see if her grandmother was around.

She flushed, washed, and brushed hair and teeth. And then realized she was starving. As if on cue, Macie heard Aunt Julie calling out to her.

"Macie, if you're hungry I've got food on the table."

Oh, sweet relief. Aunt Julie was here. Saved from Gran and from any questions that she wasn't sure she could answer anyway.

Last night's scene flooded her mind again and she didn't know if she was ever going to make sense of it all. She walked slowly down the stairs and quietly slipped into the kitchen. Aunt Julie was getting orange juice from the refrigerator and she turned as Macie was pulling out the chair from the table.

Before she could sit down, Aunt Julie had crossed the kitchen and wrapped her arms around Macie.

"I love you so much, honey. I've been checking on you all day. I was starting to get worried; you slept so long. Are you feeling okay? You didn't get sick from being outside all night, did you?"

"No, I'm fine Aunt Julie. Really, I am. I guess I was just that tired."

"Are you hungry? I made breakfast. There's french toast and scrambled eggs. I've got bacon frying, too." Aunt Julie's version of frying was a paper towel-covered plate in the microwave. It smelled just as good as cooking on the stove and Macie heard her stomach rumble.

"I'm starving. Hope you made a bunch. She asked, "How is Annie? Has anyone heard anything?"

"Carol called about an hour ago. She said they were with Annie at Children's Hospital. They gave her some fluids and watched her for several hours, but she seems just fine. Carol thought they might actually let Annie come home later this afternoon. If not today, she'll be released tomorrow morning. The doctors said she was very lucky with no broken bones or any other injuries."

"Oh, Aunt Julie, I'm so happy she's not hurt. What if she had been in there for days? What if I had been wrong? I might be in trouble, but I had to help her!" Macie's voice suddenly lowered to a whisper, "Aunt Julie?"

Aunt Julie paused with her fork in mid-air. "Yes, Macie?"

"Would you think I am crazy if I told you Annie knew I was coming to get her? She told me. Last night, right before they took her away."

"Stranger things have happened. Maybe she had a feeling about you while she was down there."

"Her exact words were 'I knew you would come when I called.'"

Aunt Julie poured more orange juice for each of them. She placed the pitcher back on the table. She looked into Macie's eyes while she spoke. "I'd say that is something very special. Not too many people get to have that kind of connection, do they?"

"No, I guess they don't. I always thought Annie was the nicest girl in our class. I just didn't think she would want to be friends with someone like me." Macie sighed, thinking about all of the times Annie had smiled at her. Maybe it wasn't because she thought Macie was odd or uncool. Or motherless. Maybe she had been smiling because she knew they could be friends.

"I'd say you definitely found a friend this time. In more ways than one, for sure."

Macie laughed a little. "I guess I did, didn't I? I can't wait to talk to her. I have to know how she even thought to call out to me. Why me? Why not someone in her family? How could she know I would hear her, see her? Did she know I was dreaming it? I have so many things I want to talk with her about. What if I tell her I dreamed it and that she was a dancer on a trophy and she thinks that I'm weird?"

"I don't think you will have to worry about that. She is so happy that you came looking for her and she was rescued, that she won't care how or why."

"I guess not. I hope not. It's too bad that I'll probably be grounded now that I might be able to talk and hang out with a friend."

"I think, at least I hope, your dad isn't going to be too angry with you. I told him he should have listened to you right away and then you wouldn't have felt you had to do it on your own. He used to do the same thing to your mom, if that makes you feel any better. He's trying. He's got some rules for you now, though."

"Oh, great! More rules. At least he might not be too hard on me. I am sorry that I ran off and scared everyone. Gran's going to be tougher, isn't she? Where is Gran, by the way?" Macie thought she needed to get her story about last night together before Gran walked in on her. "She's angry, I'll bet."

Aunt Julie paused then said very matter of fact, "She's out with some of her old friends. Your grandmother is upset with just about everyone right now. And, yes, that includes you."

"She's mad that I went past Turnback Alley even though she's warned me hundreds of times not to do that, right?"

Aunt Julie nodded. "Yes. And that you took Vanity out. And that it was dark. That you didn't wait for someone to come help you. That you hung up on your father. That you listened to a dream. That you followed that dream and it turned out to be right. Oh, she's even upset that you didn't lock the door when you left. Should I keep going? Her list gets longer."

"No. I get it. Why is she angry with everyone else?"

"She's upset with your dad because he should have prevented this somehow. She's angry with me for not making you come right home right when I found you. She's irritated that I allowed you to keep going in the woods even though we . . ."

Macie interrupted her, "We found Annie! She's upset that we saved someone from being scared and trapped and cold and afraid? Maybe even from dying. Had you tried to make me go home, I wouldn't have listened. I knew. I knew once I got into the woods that the dream had given me all the pictures I needed to find Annie."

"I know. Maybe after the dust clears and we see what happens, Gran will settle down a bit. Don't count on it though. She hates this stuff. She has for a long time."

"I don't understand." Macie had a gut feeling that there was a big story behind it.

"I'll give you the short version for now. I promise one day I will tell you more. Gran hates dreams and anything that people say they just 'feel' or know. She hates it when they act on those feelings. She is sure that when you are wrong about the feelings and dreams and little nudges that you get, it causes bad things to happen. She thinks that we should let science and her version of logic answer all of our questions. To Gran, people who let instinct and gut feelings and any sort of visions, including dreams, direct their actions are flighty and asking for trouble. She believes that kind of knowledge can only come from some place or thing that is bad."

"But you said it wasn't!"

"Your grandmother and I do not agree on this issue. And we don't talk about it, ever. I know how she feels and she knows I think differently. As long as she doesn't see it or hear about it, we get along fine."

"So what should I say to Gran, then? Wow, what am I going to say at school? What if anyone asks us what happened? Do people know I'm the one that knew where to find Annie?"

"My advice about Gran would be to not discuss last night around Gran unless she asks you about it and you feel like saying anything. Just don't be rude or disrespectful to her opinions. Let your dad deal with fielding any questions about what happened for now. He already handled the EMT and search party by telling them you were out with Gran doing work on the fields earlier in the day. He told them you realized when you saw his note that you'd heard Annie instead of what you originally thought was an animal in the woods. Luckily, he called me to check on you as soon as you hung up on him. I told him about the conversation we had in the car. Once he heard your story from me, I think he realized he made a mistake in not finding a way to listen to you without worrying what everyone would think of him and you. Once he understood how specific your dream was, he used quick thinking to bring the search party to the right place without anyone thinking it was odd."

"Do you think that's what I should say in school? That I heard something in the woods and realized it was Annie since her grandparents live on the backside of Gran's farm?" She decided for herself, "I'll have to talk to Annie and tell her." Macie felt a bit calmer with a plan. She wasn't sure she was ready to tell the world a dream guided her to Annie. "That feels like the right plan."

"Well then, I guess you already have your answer."

Chapter 18

The phone rang at 7:30 that night. Macie's stomach lurched as she called out, "I'll get it." In her mind she said, it's for me, anyway. Annie's voice was on the other end.

"Hi, Macie. It's Annie."

"Hi."

There was a long pause as both girls struggled to know what to say next.

Macie burst out, "What were you doing alone in the woods, Annie? Are you crazy?"

Quite a way to greet someone who could have died, she thought. Smart, Macie. Real smart. She cringed at her lack of tact and her apparent inability to keep a friend.

Annie laughed a nervous giggle and then quietly said, "I was looking for you."

"Me? Why me?" Macie was clueless.

"Well, I ended up at my grandparents this weekend. I started thinking about how it would be nice to have someone to talk to and I remembered that I told my mom about you coming to our school and she had said you were staying at your grandmother's house. The way she told it, our grandparents live right next to each other. No one ever said there were all those woods in between the houses. All I could think about was how nice it would be to talk to you after seeing you in school all the time. I headed out through the field figuring I could see if you were home and then get back to my Grandma's house before dinner. I take walks there all the time. But, once I into the deeper part of the forest there were so many trees and I started to lose my way. I wasn't even sure I was heading in the right direction. And then . . ."

Annie didn't continue. Macie knew then she must have fallen in that sinkhole. The rest was history.

Macie interjected, "Then you went and got yourself stuck?"

"Pretty much. I got heck from my Grandma for that. She said I should have known better than to wander off and try to visit someone's house without clearing it with her or having an invitation first. I was just so bored there this time. She was busy baking stuff for a fundraiser and Pap was out looking at a new tractor. When you popped into my mind, I just went with it and started walking."

"So, I guess it's my fault that you got yourself lost and stranded then, isn't it? Jeez, Annie. I'm sorry. I didn't even realize you would want to talk to me at all, and not during school."

"I don't think it's your fault at all! I was the stupid one who could have just asked for the phone number and called you. Sometimes, I get something in my head and I don't know what comes over me. And really, if it wasn't for you, who knows if I'd have been found at all. You saved the day."

Macie couldn't let herself just take the praise. She said, "Annie, there were tons of people searching for you. Someone would have checked the woods. They would have had to think of that and started looking in all the places around your grandparents house."

Annie wasn't convinced and she told Macie, "I don't know about that. Grandma says they just never thought I'd be," she changed her voice to sound older, mimicking her grandmother, "so adventurous to walk alone that far into the woods on my own." They won't say what they thought happened to me, but I think they figured someone kidnapped me. And I didn't tell them this part, but I started to not be able to feel my feet. Then my legs started to go numb. I kept thinking that by the time someone did find me, I wasn't going to be able to walk, or dance, ever again."

Stunned, Macie empathized, "Oh my, Annie. What a horrible feeling. And to be stuck there thinking that. It must have been so scary."

Annie recounted, "It wasn't at first. You know, I just thought someone would surely realize I was missing and would hear me calling out. I yelled and yelled while I could and then my throat got sore."

Macie interrupted, "Did you say dance? That you wouldn't be able to dance again?" Her whole body started buzzing. She felt like she was about to find the missing puzzle piece.

"Yeah, I kept thinking how awful it was to be there and how tight the space was. I really wanted to move around and couldn't. I've been taking dance since I was three and got picked for a competition team this year. I kept hoping that I'd be able to feel that kind of freedom again. I was afraid I would miss out on dancing with them and winning the big trophy."

Macie hesitated before opening up. She wondered if Annie would think her a freak if she told her how she found her. One deep breath and she went for it.

"That's how I found you. I had dreams of being called and when I went to the place in my dream that held the voice, all I could see was this trophy with a dancer on top."

"Really? You saw that? That is so cool, Macie. I felt it in school, that there was more about you that I was meant to find. That I might finally have a friend that could understand me like no one else can. I was serious when I said I knew you would come when I called. I thought it meant when I called out loud, but it must have come to you in your dream. Whatever it was, I felt that if I kept saying your name you would hear me."

Macie breathed a sigh of relief. "So, you don't think I'm weird or crazy?"

"Macie, I could never think that. If I did, then I would have to think I am too. I told you, I get something in my head and I don't know what happens to me. Well, I get all sorts of things in my head and some of them can't be explained, but they always mean something and usually lead me to something I'm supposed to know or to do. I don't know what it is or why it happens exactly, but it's there. Mom says we all have certain special abilities and that some of us believe in them more than others so we get to use them more often."

It was all too much for Macie. To think that a frustrating and slightly off the wall dream had led her to another person like her had her mind racing. She wanted to ask so many more questions and compare stories to see where Annie was going with all of this, but that would have to wait.

Macie started to ask Annie how long she felt that way, but Annie asked her to hold on a minute while she talked to her mother.

Annie came back on the line and said, "My mom's telling me I need to rest if I want to go to school tomorrow. Annie continued, "They let me come home tonight after I ate dinner, instead of making me wait until the morning. The doctors all said I was fine. Thank goodness my mom brought my writing assignment in for me to do. The docs all wanted to keep me overnight, but when they saw me doing homework and then read what I wrote, they changed their minds. This is one time I have to thank mom for making me do work."

"Annie, I'm just so happy you're okay. It's weird, isn't it? Last week I felt like I'd never have a friend in the world again and today I'm lucky to have found one." She hoped, at least, that this was the beginning of a friendship.

Annie captured Macie's feeling and then continued, "Not just found a friend; you found and saved me," And that did it. Theirs would be a forever bond.

Macie had a thought, "You know, people will think we are crazy if we tell them about the dream and trophy and other stuff."

"That's exactly what I thought!" Annie answered. "Let's not tell anyone for now."

"Ok, good. I'm not ready to explain that to other people." Macie went on, "My dad told everyone I heard you earlier in the day while I was helping my Gran, but didn't figure out it was you, and not some kind of animal, until later when we found out you were missing. If we have to say anything, I think we should go with that. It's almost the whole truth, minus the dreaming part."

Annie loved the plan. "That's a nice and simple story. I wouldn't really want tell anyone, anyway. They wouldn't understand. Macie, I knew you were coming. At least, I was really sure I did; I hoped I did, but I was really scared while I was down there. There were bugs and stuff, too." She shifted topics. "I have to go. Mom's giving me the get-off-the-phone eyes. So, do you want to meet me in the cafeteria for breakfast in the morning before we go to class?"

Macie smiled a big smile. "That would be great!"

"Do you have a brown skirt, by the way?"

Macie giggled, "You're too funny, from bugs to lunch to skirts. Although, I did just buy a brown skirt at the mall with my aunt. And cute little boots to go with it."

Annie giggled, this time with all the spirit of a youthful girl. "Cool. I just got boots to match my skirt. Let's wear them tomorrow. What kind of shirt should we wear?" Hearing them talk was like listening to girls who had been friends forever.

Deciding to wear brown and pink shirts with a pink tee underneath, their wardrobe was all set.

Macie could hear Annie's mom's voice in the background and then Annie told her, "Hey, I've got to go for real this time. Mom's giving me the look right now." She said 'the look' with a deep, drawn out voice. "Don't forget to meet me in the morning."

"I won't. See you then. I can't wait for school now." Macie hadn't said that in a very long time. She was pleasantly surprised and liked the feeling. "Tell your mom I said hi."

"I will. You're her hero right now. But, you might not be any more if we don't get off the phone."

"Okay. 'Bye. See you tomorrow."

"See you tomorrow."

Macie heard the click on the other end of the line and placed the handset in the base.

She checked in with her dad and told him, "I'm going up to get my clothes together for school. I might read for a half-hour before bed, if you don't mind."

"Nope. Go ahead, kiddo. As long as I know where you are, I'm fine." He tousled her hair. They had already talked about her new rules about sharing dreams and not going off alone again. He promised to listen much better about them. Gran was noticeably absent tonight, having decided to meet some of her friends who were going to play canasta, whatever that was.

Macie went to her room and picked one of her favorite books to read. Then she saw her new journal begging to hear the end to the big entry of the week. Mismatched socks and missed witnesses were starting to unravel a mystery, but the latest event in her dream timeline still needed told.

She thought about it all as she wrote, her fingers cramping at times making her wish she had her own computer to keep track of the dreams that had begun to guide her. All the angst over how frustrating dreams could be came to mind. It's as if you think something isn't what it seems to be only to find out it was exactly as you were shown all along. That trophy, she wrote, didn't mean anything to me until I found out the connection to Annie. Now it makes perfect sense. But, how are you supposed to know what something means, if you don't know someone that well? Even the pacing I saw in the dream with Dad was confusing. I know what he does, but didn't know that's how he gets ready for a trial. What good is a dream that gives you information that can be twisted and misinterpreted?

She analyzed parts of her dream, sticking with the things she saw clearly and what they ended up meaning. She looked over what she had written before she ran off to find Annie. She also concentrated on the images that had come together to bring her to Annie. What if I had known this wasn't just a dream, but more of a map to find something when I was awake? Why can't it just start off with a signal of some kind to let me know it's something that will really happen?

She tried to trace back through everything she wrote up to the point about the exact number of steps in her dream about Annie. She wondered if it was possible she only had the dream because Annie was reaching out to her. Then, she quite literally banged her head with the journal. She groaned, not in pain, but in frustration.

She wrote on. I wonder if it gets easier with more dreams? If I keep having them, will I get better at figuring them out? Is dreaming of something like what happened to Annie going to happen to me again? She paused in her writing at that thought. The important thing is that nothing bad happened to Annie. In the end, it doesn't matter if something that big comes in a dream again or not, she wrote. But, whatever the dreams bring from now on, I'll pay more attention to what they are telling me.

It occurred to her that in her most recent dreams two things were constant. The first was that the way she saw the pictures in the dream were very lifelike and defined, even when they didn't make sense to her. The second was that she remembered details that she ordinarily dismissed or forgot once she woke from other dreams. Her last note to herself was to start writing down all of her dreams, even if it was just a small piece that she retained once she woke.

Macie rationalized to herself. If I'm going to figure out what's different and when I should be paying attention to certain ones, I better figure out what makes a dream more than a dream. She closed the journal with a nudge in the pit of her stomach. The thought entered her mind that she HAD known the dream was different and that she had felt it was trying to tell her something all along.

She was tired now, even though she had slept most of the day. She picked up the book she'd planned to read but gave up after she read the second paragraph four times and still couldn't remember what it said. She rushed through her night routine, found her dad still on the couch and said goodnight.

"Sweet dreams, Macie." He gave her a big hug and kissed her nose.

"Hope so," she said as she headed up the stairs.

Macie's night was filled with dreams of her mother. They went for a walk in a garden, smelling flowers and soaking in the warmth of the sun. They stopped at a Willow tree on the water's edge and sat by the river. They shared memories and talked with each other. They hugged each other. Her mother even painted a picture of a wooded area with cabins numbered by Roman numerals set amidst picnic tables overlooking boats on the lake. Above it she painted a rainbow. To Macie, it felt as if she had spent a real day hanging out with her mother. Her mother smiled and hugged her when it was time to go.

Macie's alarm clock broke into the dream, but Macie woke happy and thankful for the time with her mom. She put on her new outfit and boots. She combed her hair and found a brown headband to slide over it. She grabbed her book bag as she left her room.

Heading to the kitchen with a huge smile on her face, she was excited for school. She had already told dad she wanted to eat breakfast at school, so she sat and waited for James to finish his. They headed out the door with plenty of time to spare. When the bus came, James said he wanted to sit with his new friend Brian, whom he had found the day before when Macie wasn't there.

Macie was a little nervous as she stepped on the bus, but smiled when one of the girls in the other fifth grade class called out for her.

"Macie. Over here! Do you want to sit with me?" Teana Bartwell motioned to her seat. "Your brother is sitting with my cousin."

"Sure." Macie slid in beside her and let her book bag rest between her feet.

"Everyone was talking about you in school yesterday. You and Annie. Is it true you helped find her?" Teana immediately slapped her hand over her mouth. "Oh, there I go. My mom said I should stop being so nosy."

Macie laughed, but was glad the ride to school wasn't very long. "It's okay. Yeah, I guess I helped find her. She's coming back to school today."

"Really? So soon? Good! You guys are so cool." Teana didn't stop talking until the bus pulled in front of the school.

Macie headed straight for the cafeteria. She wasn't sure how breakfast worked because she normally ate at home and had never joined the breakfast crowd. Annie, Robbie and a few others were just entering the cafeteria doors. Annie grabbed Macie's arm as they headed for the line. Once they were in place they gave a quick hug. You couldn't go through something as crazy and wondrous as they had and not feel the need to connect. The day felt right already.

They ate quickly and talked in between bites so they wouldn't miss the bell. They admired each other's outfits and were happy with how close of a match the clothes were. There wasn't much time to talk before the first bell rang. Annie and Macie said they'd save each other a seat at lunch as they headed up the hall to Mrs. Rich's room. It was going to feel like forever until they got to talk at lunch.

They giggled all the way up the hall with Robbie and Teana, who had joined them on the way to her own classroom.

Macie walked into the room with her new best friend, happier than any of her class mates had ever seen her. Penny ignored her after giving her a look that said she did not think much of the newly proclaimed hero of the school. The cryptic note that Maya passed her when Penny wasn't looking told all and yet told nothing.

Your dad put Penny's uncle in jail.

Even though it caused her body temperature to heat up and the pit of her stomach to drop, that piece of news would have to wait until she got home. For now, the morning flew by and even missing a day of school didn't keep her from having a perfect spelling pretest and math quiz.

In computer class, she and Annie sat by one another. Mrs. Rich stopped in to check Annie's and then Macie's writing assignment. She told Macie it was wonderful writing. "Those are great visuals you chose. You can type that just the way it is, Macie. I wouldn't change a thing."

"Neither would I, Mrs. Rich," Macie said with a twinkle in her eye.

Macie thought of how much she had wanted to find a friend. She knew that she had found a best friend in Annie. She knew they were going to share gifts that did not come wrapped in birthday paper or get placed under a tree.

They were going to have lots of chances to find out how similar they really were. And how different they really might be from other kids. Of course, that was just a feeling. Something that had come to her in a dream. She told herself she couldn't really be sure of the future. Or could she?

Macie Graye

Language Arts

5th Grade—Mrs. Rich

The Perfect Day

On my perfect day, I wake up after having the best dream I have ever had. In the dream, my mother and I have spent a day talking and having fun. I can feel her kisses and hugs. Her smile is as beautiful as I remember it and it makes me feel safe and warm. It helps me to not be so sad, even though I miss her just as much as always.

Today, I look forward to school as I get dressed. I'm not worried or anxious that people will think I am strange or only be nice to me because I am the girl without a mother. Or not be nice to me because I am different. Today I won't hide from anyone out of fear that they will ask me about my mom and make me start crying.

On my perfect day, I will fit in, not because I have the right clothes or clothes like everyone else. I will fit in because I know what I like and feel like I can share those things with friends. My bag is packed and my new outfit fits perfectly. I am on time this morning and even early for the bus.

When I get on the bus, no one looks at me like I am an alien. Someone has saved me a seat and calls out my name. On my perfect day, people will like me for who I am.

I'm not afraid of being alone on this day. A group of new friends is waiting for me. We talk and laugh and it makes me feel as if I finally belong here. This day will be perfect because no one will see me as an outcast for being scared and alone. On my perfect day, I get to hear what other kids worry about doing or saying or feeling and try to help them.

I get through all my classes and make all A's, not because I deserve them, but because I've earned them.

Lunch is a great time today because I have a best friend who saves me a seat at the table. We have the most fun, sharing secrets and talking about music and movies, clothes and teachers, and maybe even something that is really important to the world.

During my perfect day, no one makes fun of me. If anyone did, my new friends would stick up for me. The other kids don't giggle behind my back. And maybe it will be so perfect that even if they did, I just wouldn't even care.

On my perfect day it will be okay to be sad that my mom is gone and feel happiness for other things at the same time.

On my perfect day, I am happy to be me again.

CPSIA information can be obtained at www.ICGtesting.com
Printed in the USA
BVOW022138280312

286328BV00003B/3/P